KILLER SPECIES
out for blood

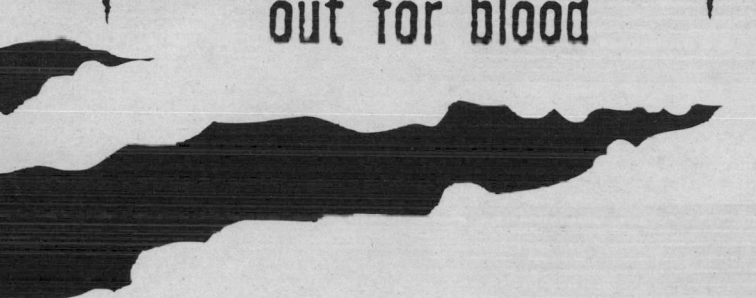

KILLER SPECIES
out for blood

Michael P. Spradlin

SCHOLASTIC INC.

ISBN 978-0-545-50676-2

12 11 10 9 8 7 6 5 4 3 2   14 15 16 17 18 19/0

Printed in the U.S.A.   40
This edition first printing, March 2014

The display type was set in Badhouse Light.
The text type was set in Apollo MT.
Book design by Nina Goffi

To Christopher Moore.
Because, you know, monsters and stuff . . .

KILLER SPECIES
out for blood

Prologue

IT HAD COME TO THIS.

Dr. Catalyst piloted the boat silently through the Aerojet Canal outside of Florida City. It was nearing midnight, and the sky was full of rain clouds. He was moving through the water on low power with no lights. Though capture was unlikely, he was still a wanted fugitive and took every precaution.

His advance planning and well-reasoned strategies had led him to this moment. A few weeks ago, his latest efforts at combating the invasive species infesting South Florida had been thwarted again by Emmet Doyle and Calvin Geaux. Dr. Catalyst glanced down at his mangled right hand, something else he had Emmet and Calvin to thank for. In the Everglades, Emmet had induced a

Pterogator to attack him, and its bite had nearly severed his arm. Now he had lost access to his Pterogators and Muraecudas. And not only that, Emmet's stupid dog had bitten him. Repeatedly. He was tired, aching, and angry.

Dr. Catalyst was through with subtlety. He was finished with taking a measured approach. Those in power did not see the value of his methods. Man had introduced vile, destructive creatures into the fragile ecosystem and the only way to heal it was to create a new level of predators to eliminate them. All he was asking was to be left alone to save the environment.

The boat slowed to a stop, floating gently in the middle of the canal. A few weeks ago, he had come to this very spot to kidnap Emmet Doyle's dog, Apollo. The Doyle home backed up to the canal and was close to the Everglades. Remembering that night made his bitten calf muscle ache, reminding him of his failure.

On the boat's rear deck was a large Plexiglas construct, roughly the size of a phone booth. Small holes were drilled in the sides to allow in oxygen for the creatures inside. Dr. Catalyst put on a helmet with a clear plastic face shield. He was wearing thick gloves and canvas coveralls. As he approached the container, the animals within it flapped leathery wings and a chittering rose from inside.

He placed his gloved hands on the clear plastic, and the captured creatures swarmed at them, thumping against the side. Loud screeching sounds replaced the chittering. Dr. Catalyst could make out one of the creatures in the din, flapping wings with long, pointed claws at their end. Its face was a horror of small, sharp teeth and huge, dark eyes, plus a pair of insectlike antennae. The creature's wings tucked in as it stretched toward him, revealing not four spindly limbs, but six. There were hundreds just like it in the container. They were small in size, but very belligerent. Each one weighed only a few ounces, and their wingspans were less than a foot long when fully extended. A swarming, squirming, buzzing mass of hungry terror.

Unbelievably hungry.

Once again he had combined two separate species. Each was aggressive in its own right. The vampire bat was a nocturnal hunter that required drinking over 60 percent of its body weight in mammalian blood each night in order to survive. The baldfaced hornet was among the most aggressive members of the yellow-jacket family. They could bite as well as sting, and protected their nests with the utmost ferocity. With his revolutionary gene-splicing, growth hormones, and his technique for recombining DNA from divergent species, Dr. Catalyst had created the ideal invasive species.

Yes.

An invasive species.

He was releasing his own nonnative animals into South Florida. His Pterogators and Muraecudas had served a specific purpose: to rid the Everglades and the ocean of snakes and lionfish.

But his newest creations — he was going to call them Blood Jackets — were here for only one reason: to create havoc.

If no one would willingly accept his methods, he would show them the negative impact of an invasive species firsthand. And before long his latest creations would find sustenance from the most prevalent warm-blooded mammals in Florida.

Humans.

Dr. Catalyst stepped inside the cabin of the boat. He had rigged a cable release, attached to a pulley system, which allowed the creatures to be set free from inside, where it was safe. Still, he wore the helmet and thick coveralls as a precaution.

Taking a breath, he pushed a lever forward, and through a hole drilled in the cabin wall, the cable pulled open the top of the cage. For a moment, nothing happened. Then, with a rush of wings and loud piercing squeals, they exploded into the night sky. Dozens of the creatures threw themselves at the cabin window, then more followed, trying to reach him through the glass. Their savageness caused Dr. Catalyst to draw back from the sight of them. Unable to breach the cabin, they finally gave up and flew upward, joining hundreds of their brethren in the sky.

From here they would spread out and begin nesting. Colonies would form and they would terrorize the population of Florida City.

They would own the night.

1

THE THING ABOUT DOGS IS THEY EAT A LOT, SLEEP A LOT, and if they were Apollo — with a sense of smell and hearing he considered superior to every living creature, including other dogs — they were sometimes obsessive about needing to go outside. Ever since he was taken captive by Dr. Catalyst, Apollo woke up several times a night, wanting to investigate the backyard. It was as if he had a score to settle with his onetime captor.

It was almost midnight, according to the clock on the bedroom desk. Apollo was standing on Emmet's chest, licking his face and making a soft growling sound. Emmet tried rolling over and burying himself with pillows and blankets. No use. Apollo dug through and found Emmet's face again, where he went to work licking and yipping quietly. Either he had to go, or he'd heard something outside that needed investigation. And Emmet would get no rest until Apollo was sure the backyard was secure.

Sitting up, Emmet rubbed the sleep from his eyes. Apollo sat back on his haunches, pleased that Emmet now understood what was required of him. He ran his hand over Apollo's ears and scratched gently. Next to food of nearly any kind, this was the dog's most favorite thing. Emmet felt Apollo's collar, making sure it was securely attached, and checking the special dog-license medallion attached to it.

After Dr. Catalyst kidnapped Apollo, Dr. Geaux had gone to the FBI and obtained a unique fob for Apollo's license. It looked like a regular dog license, but it contained a special chip in it that would allow them to track Apollo, were he to be captured again.

"I don't suppose I could talk you out of this, could I?" Emmet whispered. Apollo cocked his head and gave a quiet yip.

"Couldn't you at least bark loud enough to wake up Dad? Then *he* could take you outside," Emmet grumbled. "Come on."

He stood up, stretched, and stumbled groggily for his bedroom door. Outside he heard thunder rumble off in the distance. A storm must be coming. The wind was making a weird noise on the roof of the house. It sounded like — Emmet wasn't sure at first — like a humming, buzzing sound. Or maybe it was flapping. Could be the shingles were loose or something. He was too tired to pay much attention. Apollo ran ahead of him to the back door and scratched at it eagerly.

"Hold your horses," Emmet groused. "You shouldn't drink so much water before you go to bed. I've got school tomorrow, you know. I need my beauty rest."

There was a brand-new alarm-system pad next to the door. Emmet entered the code and it beeped as it was deactivated. When he opened the door, Apollo catapulted through it and rushed across the small stone patio to the grass, nose down, sniffing the ground like a bloodhound. Emmet often wondered what it must be like to have the millions of scents in the world pulling you in a different direction every few seconds.

Ever since Dr. Catalyst had snatched Apollo, Emmet stood in the doorway and watched over him while he was outside. He still had nightmares and horrible flashbacks of Apollo tumbling into the tank full of Muraecudas. He was determined that the madman would never get his hands on Apollo again, so the little black mutt got a wingman whenever he had to visit the backyard.

Apollo sniffed his way along the ground to the first of the three cypress trees that grew in the yard. Emmet watched him through hooded eyes, still groggy with sleep. The wind picked up, and off to the west the sky brightened as fingers of lightning reached out of the clouds. Over the breeze, he heard that weird buzzing, flapping sound above his head again. For a moment he thought it sounded like bird wings. *I need sleep,* Emmet thought. *Hurry up, Apollo.*

Now the dog was sniffing hard at the base of the tree. He went up on his hind legs, his forepaws planted against the trunk of the tree. Emmet groaned. He hoped it wasn't a raccoon. He could be out here all night. He flipped on the outdoor lights.

"Apollo, come," he said. Apollo ignored the command.

And barked. Loudly.

"Apollo," Emmet hissed. "Quiet! Come on, let's go!"

Apollo was unmoved.

Emmet left the doorway, the screen door slamming behind him, and trotted to the tree. Apollo darted away.

"Oh, come on!" Emmet complained. The strange noise grew louder now that he was outside in the yard. From the corner of his eye, he thought he saw something dark fly low across the ground, from the tree toward the roof of the house. It must have been a bird. Nothing drove Apollo nuts like birds.

While he was chasing Apollo, another bird flew from

the tree to the roof, and Apollo pursued it. When Emmet turned around to follow his dog, he suddenly saw that the roof of their house was covered with birds. They were flapping their wings and hopping about, and the bizarre chittering sound was coming from them. Florida had hundreds of bird species. Nighttime was a symphony of animal noises, from birds to frogs to alligators bellowing in the canal behind their house. But he had yet to hear the call of this one. To Emmet it sounded almost like bees in a hive. Maybe it was some kind of seasonal migration no one had bothered to warn him about.

As he trailed Apollo toward the house, the sound changed from a low-pitched hum to a high screech. Emmet skidded to a stop in the yard. Apollo was in a barking frenzy. Now that he was close enough to see the roof clearly in the light, Emmet froze in fear.

These were not birds roosting on the rooftop of their house.

They were bats.

A whole lot of bats. Hundreds of them. And as Emmet shouted in alarm, they rose as one into the night sky, wings flapping with a furious and impossible speed, a horrible shriek rising over the noise of the wind. Terrified, Emmet wanted to run but was rooted in place.

"Dad! Dad! Hurry!" he shouted as loud as he could.

The bats circled briefly in the air above him. Then, like something out of the most frightening horror movie he had ever seen, they turned in flight.

And they dived directly toward him.

2

"**D**AD! HELP! DAD!" EMMET YELLED, BUT HIS SHOUTS were quelled by the horrific sound of flapping leathery wings and the screech of hundreds of bats flying at him. The air around him was full of teeth and fur and noise. One minute he was ten yards away from the back door of his house, and the next he couldn't see through the mass of writhing creatures. He had no idea in which direction he would find safety.

Apollo howled and charged toward Emmet, snapping and growling as the bats attacked his master. Finally catching sight of the back-door lights, Emmet was able to orient himself, but it was impossible for him to take even a single step against the onslaught.

"Emmet!" Dr. Doyle's voice cut through the pandemonium. "Hold on, son!"

All Emmet could think to do was fall to the ground. Landing on his hands and knees, he grabbed Apollo and pulled him beneath his chest. The dog was not happy to be taken out of the fight, and tried to wiggle his way free. Emmet couldn't tell if he was being stung or bitten, but sharp pricks of pain stabbed at his arms and neck.

He felt something suddenly grip his arm and lift him to his feet. Emmet just hoped it was his dad, and not a giant bat that was going to carry him off into the night.

"Come on!" his dad shouted. He was viciously swinging a broom through the air with his other hand, swatting the creatures out of the sky. Emmet held tightly to the struggling Apollo as his father guided them through the swirling horde.

Emmet felt funny. His skin hurt and stung all around his neck, face, and arms. He felt himself stumbling and tightened his grip on his dad's arm as they crashed through the screen door into the kitchen, landing in a heap on the floor. Dr. Doyle clambered to his feet, still swinging the broom at the two bats that had followed them into the kitchen through the broken screen.

Emmet wanted to stand up, but he felt dizzy and a little nauseous. He wondered if the bites contained some kind of venom. When he looked at his hands and arms, he saw they were bleeding and swollen. He tried rising from the floor, but Apollo was jumping and barking at a couple of the bats that were circling the kitchen. The noise of the whirring, biting mass of chaos had made him woozy and disoriented.

Dr. Doyle slammed the back door shut, and there were several *thumps* against the wooden barrier.

"Hey, buddy!" his dad said. "Can you stand up?"

Emmet wanted to answer him, but his tongue felt thick and goofy. It didn't seem to want to work right. He wanted to say, "I think so," but it came out, "My sheep slow." Emmet's head flopped back onto the floor, and it hurt. His whole body throbbed with pain.

Lying on his back, he could see two of the creatures perched on the kitchen light fixture. Apollo barked furiously at them. Emmet felt his father lifting him up and carrying him into the front room of their house. His eyes felt strange, and he was having trouble seeing, like they might be swollen shut or something.

"Hang on, buddy," his dad said, laying him on the sofa. "Come on, Apollo!"

Apollo jumped up on the couch and started licking Emmet's face. It tickled, but Emmet couldn't say anything to get him to stop. His dad slammed the door shut, closing them off from the kitchen. Behind him, two loud *thump*s issued out as the creatures smacked against it.

The last thing Emmet remembered was his father's voice.

"Hello? 9-1-1? We need an ambulance! Hurry!"

3

IT TOOK SEVERAL HOURS IN ALL, BUT DR. CATALYST released four more containers of his Blood Jackets into the wild at various locations around Florida City. He suspected there were now at least two thousand free in the night sky. It would be difficult to determine what impact they might have on the ecosystem, but at this point he no longer cared. These creatures were voracious feeders and would be difficult to catch. They would occupy the time and resources of those who pursued him, leaving him free to continue his gallant struggle.

The animals swarmed through the darkening sky. Their first instinct would be to find a place to nest and grow the colony. Once they found a secure home in which to spend the daylight hours, with access to a freshwater source, hunting would begin. The resulting terror would overtake the city, and he would finally be free to complete his work.

Dr. Catalyst watched the last group fly off into the darkness from the safety of the boat's cabin. They were a magnificent species. It had been a much bigger scientific challenge creating these hybrids. The species that he crossed to breed his Pterogators and Muraecudas shared common evolutionary and genetic ancestors. Vampire bats and baldfaced hornets were from two entirely different classes: mammal and insect. Despite this, there were similarities in their behavior. Bat colonies and hornet hives were alike in that each member had different roles and duties. Vampire bats shared blood with colony members to sustain their numbers. Hornets were highly protective of their nest and the queen. Regardless of how difficult it was, Dr. Catalyst was so brilliant that he had made it work.

Now it was time to watch them in action.

The first colony released that night found a home in the steeple of a church not far from the Florida City downtown area. The vented structure was high above the building and offered easy access in and out. It was also near several residential areas, which would offer plenty of food sources.

Two of the colonies found refuge in deserted warehouses in an abandoned industrial park on the outskirts of Florida City. In truth, they were located too close to each other, and would soon begin fighting over territory. One of them would eventually drive the other out, forcing the refugees to find a new home. But for the first night, each building gave them shelter from the coming storm.

The fourth batch first stopped to rest on the roof of the Doyle home but, after terrorizing the Doyle family, moved on. They flew through the night behaving almost like a living cloud. Their screeching became louder and more frequent until it eventually sounded like a constant wail. Dogs barked at the sound, cats scurried for cover beneath porches and picnic tables, and people who happened to be outside at that late hour looked up, wondering what could be causing such a ruckus.

On and on they flew, occasionally pausing to rest in trees or on rooftops, but unable to find a suitable roost. The wind was getting stronger, and the first drops of rain were falling from the clouds when a single member of the colony returned to the rooftop where the others rested. Screeching, the lone Blood Jacket gave a signal to the others, who rose into the sky and followed.

From the air the building looked like a giant letter H. But at the bottom right of the structure were numerous large industrial roof vents. Several of the slats on the vents were rusted through and broken off, leaving an opening sufficient in size for the colony to venture through. The ductwork inside was perfect for nesting and offered protection from the elements and any potential predators.

The clouds opened, and as the rain fell, hundreds and hundreds of South Florida's newest invasive species entered Tasker Middle School.

4

THE NEXT THING EMMET REMEMBERED WAS brightness. A harsh light hurt his eyes, causing him to squint against the glare. When he was fully aware, he realized there was a man standing over him, shining a penlight in his eyes. Which kind of hurt. He wished the man would stop. His entire body ached. Finally, the light went away, and his father's face appeared in his field of vision.

"Hey, pal," he said. "How you holding up?"

Emmet groaned. "Like grizzlies have been using me to play badminton." As Emmet became more aware of his surroundings, he realized he felt a little sluggish. He lifted his left arm and found it was attached to an IV. His skin was covered with bandages.

When his eyes could focus better, he looked at his dad and saw his face was covered in bites and scratches.

"What happened? Where's Apollo?" Emmet asked. He tried sitting up, but dizziness overtook him and he slumped back into the bed.

"Whoa, fella," his dad said. "You're pumped full of painkillers, and as near as the doctors can tell you've been stung — repeatedly — by hornets. You've got a lot of their venom coursing through your veins right now."

"Whaa?" Emmet said. "Hornets? Wasn't it bats?"

"It was both," said a voice from the doorway. Emmet looked over to see Dr. Geaux and Calvin enter the room. "First of all, we just came from the vet hospital. Apollo is fine. He had several bites and stings as well, but he got some antivenom shots and he's being his usual bouncy self; the entire staff is in love with him. But the vet wants to keep him a couple of days to make sure he's okay and doesn't have a reaction."

Dr. Geaux moved to Emmet's bedside, placing her hand on his forehead. She leaned over and kissed him on the cheek. Emmet blushed. At least he thought he did. His face was so swollen and sore he couldn't tell for sure. Calvin came to his bed and gave him a fist bump. For Calvin, this was an expression of deep concern and an indication that he was glad his friend was okay.

"You were saying something about bats and hornets?" Emmet said. "The details are fuzzy."

"Yes. We had animal control go in and get the two remaining in your kitchen. We haven't had time to do a complete analysis, of course, but this is another hybrid species. They're most definitely some genus of vampire bat, which are nonnative to South Florida; they mostly come from tropical climates. And they appear to have been cross-replicated with a species of hornet because . . . they have stingers," Dr. Geaux said.

"You've got to be kidding," Dr. Doyle said.

"Giant teeth on Pterogators and Muraecudas wasn't enough, now he has to go for fangs *and* stingers? That's just great," Emmet said groggily.

Dr. Geaux laughed. A desperate, fed-up, I've-had-enough-of-this-guy type of laugh. "So it would appear," she said.

"And I don't suppose there's been any sign of him?" Dr. Doyle asked.

"No. But we're getting reports of bat attacks all over the city. It's daylight now and there's no current reported activity, so it looks like they're still nocturnal creatures. But last night the Florida City PD logged over thirty calls. So far only minor injuries and no fatalities. But those things have venom. And if they're part vampire bat, they probably survive by drinking blood. It's only going to be a matter of time before something really bad happens. We're going to have to put out a warning telling people to stay indoors at night until we can get a handle on these things," Dr. Geaux said.

"So we're not going to have the big long discussion over whether or not Dr. Catalyst is behind this?" Emmet said.

"No," Dr. Geaux said. "Who else would it be? You've been right all along."

"Could you say that again?" Emmet croaked. Dr. Geaux and his dad chuckled.

Emmet felt no satisfaction. After the incident with the Pterogators, Dr. Catalyst was silent for several months, and everyone had assumed he was dead. Then the Muraecudas appeared, and everyone except Emmet thought he had an accomplice or copycat working with him. But Emmet and Calvin confronted him again when he kidnapped Apollo. It was definitely the same guy.

Emmet was convinced Dr. Catalyst was actually their science teacher, Dr. Newton. But when the cops searched his apartment they found it trashed, and Newton missing. It appeared as if he'd been kidnapped. Now no one knew what to think. Except Emmet. He figured if Dr. Catalyst could fake a death in the Everglades, he could fake a kidnapping. Except for one niggling detail.

A Pterogator had crunched on Dr. Catalyst's arm out in the swamp. Both Emmet and Calvin had witnessed it. And when Calvin confronted him in the aquarium, his hand was all mangled up from tendon and nerve damage. Dr. Newton's arm was in a cast, but his hand didn't have any damage. Still, Emmet was sure he was faking it all somehow.

"I don't get it," Calvin piped up.

"Get what?" Dr. Geaux asked.

"What are these creatures for? I mean, the Pterogators were developed to combat snakes in the Glades, and the Muraecudas were created to go after lionfish. His whole crusade is about stopping invasive species. But why would he create these . . . bat-a . . ." Calvin struggled to find a term to describe the new hybrids.

"Bat-a-hornets?" Emmet offered. "And I'd say the invasive species they're combatting is pretty easy to figure out."

"What is it?" Calvin asked.

"It's us," Emmet said.

5

WHEN EMMET NEXT WOKE UP, HIS DAD AND CALVIN were still there, and this time Riley, Stuke, and Raeburn were in the room, too. Emmet's face still felt like someone had pounded on it with a croquet mallet, but he managed to wave weakly at his friends from the hospital bed.

"Wow," Stuke said. "Animals really don't like you, do they?"

"Stuke!" Riley and Raeburn said at the same time.

"What? I just meant all kinds of critters tend to show up whenever Emmet is around. Flying gators, super-eels, and now . . . whatever these are," he said.

Emmet coughed, trying not to laugh, and it made his face hurt.

"While you guys catch up, I'm going to stretch my legs and get some coffee," Dr. Doyle said. He left the room and it was just the five of them. Emmet's friends clustered around his bed.

"Stuke's sort of right. Wherever I go, monsters seem to follow," Emmet said.

"Well, geez," Raeburn said. "We're glad you're okay. It does look really painful, though. I feel sorry for you and Stuke."

A long red scar laddered with stitches ran up along Stuke's leg, where a Muraecuda had taken a big chunk out of it earlier in the year. It was all discolored and looked kind of like spoiled hamburger. Stuke was going to need a lot of plastic surgery to repair the damage. Which only made Emmet want to stake Dr. Catalyst to an anthill that much more. Stuke was still using a walker to get around while he rebuilt strength in his leg.

"What were . . . are those things?" Riley asked.

"Calvin's mom is having them checked out at the lab. But right now we're going with 'Blood Jacket.' Calvin invented it. I'm very proud of him," Emmet said. Calvin hadn't invented it at all, but Emmet liked to give Calvin credit for stuff when Riley was around.

Riley laughed and Calvin blushed.

" 'Blood Jacket'?" Raeburn said.

"Yeah, apparently Dr. *Crazylyst* mixed a vampire bat with some kind of hornet or yellow jacket. It can bite, suck your blood, *and* sting. And I'm probably going to turn into a vampire at any minute . . . so, you know . . . watch out for that," Emmet said.

"That's a myth," Raeburn said. "Vampire bats do drink blood, but usually from livestock. They almost never feed from humans. Unless you were passed out or something."

"Do you know everything?" Emmet asked, smiling.

"Pretty much," she answered.

"Whatever they are, there were a lot of them, and they were mean. And aggressive. And mean."

"You said that already," Stuke said.

"Just wanted to get my point across," Emmet said.

"So Dr. Catalyst went from big and scary to small and terrifying. Why do you suppose that is?" Riley asked.

"Emmet has a theory," Calvin said. "I was saying how I didn't see what invasive species he created the Blood Jackets to combat. And Emmet said, 'us.'"

"I did? Oh, yeah, I did, didn't I?" Emmet said.

"What do you mean, 'us'?" Stuke said. His face turned a little white and he stood up straighter.

"I don't think he's so hard to figure out," Emmet said. "He created Pterogators to eat snakes and Muraecudas to clear out the lionfish. But there's no invasive species for bats or hornets to go after. At least not an obvious one."

"Are you saying those things are going to feed on people?" Stuke asked, now clearly animated.

"Stuke . . . easy," Calvin said.

"Dr. Geaux thinks they're nocturnal. So if everyone stays inside at night, they'll be okay. But not everyone can do that. Think of people who have to work after dark. They have jobs and houses, and they can't just pick up and move. And these things are really aggressive. Eventually they're going to get really hungry and —"

"Emmet," Raeburn said, nodding her head in Stuke's direction. He was standing ramrod straight, the blood drained from his face, gripping his walker so tightly he might squeeze it in two if he wasn't careful.

"What do you think will happen?" Riley asked. "Will there be some kind of curfew or something?"

"I expect there will be," Calvin said. "My mom is meeting with the task force now."

"I wish there was something we could do," Raeburn said.

"There is," Emmet said. All four of them looked at him.

"When I get out of here, we're going to figure out where Dr. Catalyst is hiding. And then we're going to stop him."

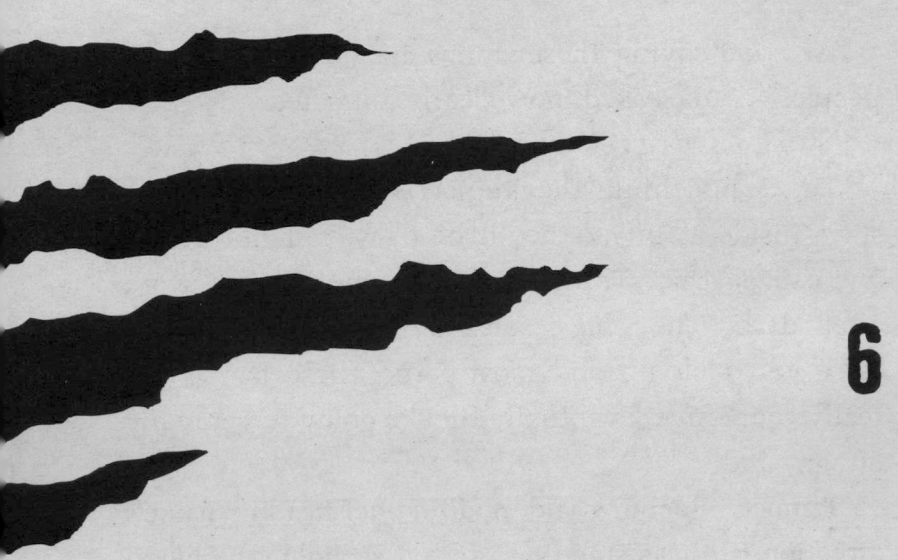

THE FOLLOWING EVENING, WHILE EMMET SLEPT IN THE hospital, Dr. Catalyst sent out his first press release. He was proud of the name: "Blood Jackets." It was meant to instill fear in those who heard it. While the news stations broadcast his message for the very first time, the creatures took to the night sky.

They hunted.

The two Dr. Geaux's team had captured alive inside Emmet's kitchen were being studied to determine their exact genetic makeup. But it would take time for blood and tissue samples to be examined, and an exact identification would not soon be forthcoming.

Dr. Catalyst's press release saved them the time. He bragged at length about the accomplishment of creating

30

a new creature from two entirely unrelated species: the vampire bat and the baldfaced hornet. In fact, he talked so much about his fantastic accomplishment that the press release was fifteen pages long. Needless to say, he was severely edited by most news outlets.

Dr. Catalyst cruised through the streets of Florida City in a late-model pickup truck. It was trash night in this part of town, and to disguise his intentions, he stopped and loaded a few old chairs and lamps and other assorted junk from the piles of stuff everyone was leaving at the curb into the bed of the vehicle. In reality, he was looking for signs of where his creations were nesting. He planned to release more colonies soon, and hoped to get a sense of the territory each group had carved out for itself. Doing so would allow him to release the next groups strategically, so they didn't encroach on one another's hunting grounds.

He had placed small transmitters on several of the members of each group. Truthfully, he was unsure how well they would work. Vampire bats were small, weighing only a few ounces, so his tracers had to be small and light enough to allow the creatures to fly. As such, they had limited power and range.

Dr. Catalyst drove slowly through the side streets and residential neighborhoods, periodically checking his tablet for any signals. But so far, nothing. Perhaps they had flown farther than he anticipated, maybe even deep within the Everglades. If so, they would be far out of range. He drove on in ever-widening circles.

While Dr. Catalyst searched, the Blood Jackets flew all around the darkened Florida City sky. It was still overcast and spitting rain, but the desire to feed drove them out in nearly any kind of weather. It wasn't long before the colony found its first victims.

On a small lake, well-known to bass fishermen in the area, two men sat in a boat, casting for fish.

A sudden screeching cry cut through the night. Both men looked up at the sound, but in the darkness and overcast sky, neither could see what had raised such a ruckus. . . .

Until they were pummeled relentlessly by hundreds of flying, stinging, biting, killing machines.

Luckily for one man, he had just stood up in the boat to cast his line. The force of the collision drove him over the side of the boat and into the water. His companion was not so lucky.

The flock battered the second fisherman to the deck of the boat. He screamed as fangs and stingers pierced his skin. The monstrous creatures bit into his arms in a frenzy, each puncture delivering a shock of burning, intense pain. He furiously waved his arms above his head, shouting desperately for help.

Suddenly, his friend's arm reached over the side of the boat from the water, jerking him into the lake with a loud splash.

The creatures swarmed at the two men's faces. "Hold your breath!" screamed the first man. They both took in air and ducked beneath the water. From below the surface, the cloud of creatures looked like a living shadow, desperately grasping and trying to reach them. As seconds bled into minutes, their lungs screaming in protest, the dark mass slowly began to dissipate.

Both men surfaced a few moments later. The fisherman who had been attacked was now barely conscious, eyes fluttering and lips a troubling blue color. With great effort, his friend finally succeeded in lifting him into the boat, then scrabbled in himself and started the engine. His friend began to moan and shake on the deck of the boat, as if he was having a seizure. He opened the throttle all the way.

He raced the boat toward shore, just hoping he could get to a hospital in time.

Meanwhile, the colony had circled back toward the city, and was now directly over a subdivision full of homes. Below them, a teenage boy pulled a trash can along his driveway toward the curb.

The creatures descended on him from the darkened

sky with frightening speed. The animals were now in a frenzy of maddening hunger, desperate to feed, and plowed into him with claws, teeth, and stingers. The boy screamed, covering his head with his arms, though the bats bit into them just as readily.

He grabbed the trash-can lid and swung it back and forth, knocking some of the creatures away. Somehow he managed to stay on his feet and sprinted back up the driveway toward his house, trailing a cloud of wings and teeth behind him.

The boy barely made it to the garage ahead of the ravenous creatures. He pounded on the button for the garage-door opener, trying to will it to close faster and screaming desperately for help. Most of the Blood Jackets flew out the door before it could close, but several remained after their escape was sealed off.

Hearing the commotion, the boy's parents opened the door to the house just in time to see their son slump to the ground, his arms bleeding and swollen, and the dozen or so creatures still in the garage diving and attacking him repeatedly.

His father charged in and grabbed a nearby baseball bat, while his mother struggled to pull the wounded boy inside the house.

Covering the two, his father swung the baseball bat at the creatures until both were safely in the door, then backed in and slammed it shut with an agonizing cry that mixed fear and gratitude that they were all still alive.

It was a long wait for the ambulance.

On the colony flew, through the night, their shrieks becoming louder as their hunger grew. They dived and darted through the sky, descending on whatever unlucky citizens of Florida City happened to be outside.

The other colonies had caused havoc as well. That night, over one hundred people would be taken to hospital emergency rooms, poisoned and bleeding.

But the colony flew south now. Their hunger, augmented by the aggressive genetic code of the hornet, demanded they be fed. So far, everything they'd hunted had managed to escape before they could take in enough blood to satisfy their need.

Until at last they rose up over a small, open tract of land. Below them, the colony spotted a field full of cattle. Diving as one, they dropped from the sky onto the unsuspecting creatures.

And they fed.

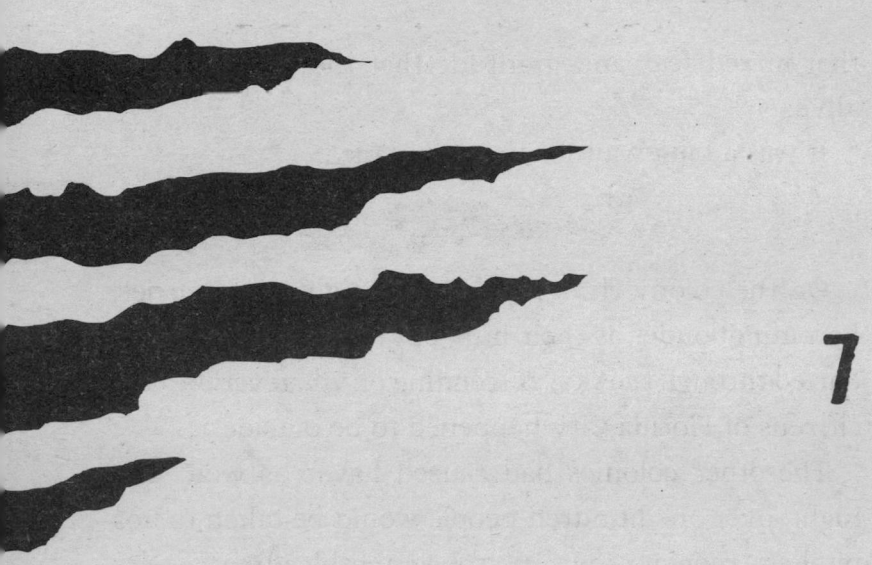

7

THE SUNLIGHT FROM THE HIGH WINDOWS CRAWLED slowly across the floor, flooding Dr. Newton's eyes. He groaned, waking slowly, the effects of the drugs used to keep him semiconscious slowing his reflexes. He was in a prison cell that had been constructed inside a large industrial warehouse, or a factory of some kind. The cell held a cot, a toilet, and a box of food. Just outside the bars sat a large watercooler, its spigot accessible inside the cell. A tin cup fastened to a chain hung from the spigot.

He knew that Dr. Catalyst had kept Dr. Doyle drugged the same way, through his water supply, back when he'd kidnapped the man.

At first Dr. Newton had tried to go without the water, hoping he'd be found or could think of a way to escape. But in Florida, thirst overcomes one quickly, and he was soon forced to drink the tainted water. The drugs made it hard to think and plot an escape.

He had no idea how long he'd been here, or if anyone was even looking for him. In fact, he only assumed it was Dr. Catalyst who had captured him — that he'd seen the plan was going sour and surprised him. Whoever captured him had managed to take him by surprise. But this wasn't the first time he'd ever been taken prisoner.

In his line of work, a man made enemies.

If Dr. Catalyst had discovered that he'd interfered with his plans in some way, he would have certainly acted.

Sitting up, he slid to the edge of the cot and tried to think. Every day he sat silent in the cell, straining to concentrate on his environment, desperate to determine where he was. There were no windows he could see out of, or sounds nearby to give any sense of a possible location. Dr. Catalyst was wealthy beyond belief, and could have any number of hideouts prepared for just such a situation.

Dr. Newton stared up at the webcam positioned outside the bars, just out of reach. He was being monitored, which made an escape attempt more difficult. Besides, the cell was impossible to break out of. The bars were in solid metal frames and bolted to the floor. His pockets were empty. There was nothing useful inside the enclosure. No way to get out.

It was safe to assume he'd been reported missing by now. Not showing up for school would have raised an alarm. Eventually his house would be searched and they would find the signs of a struggle he barely remembered.

He lay back down on the cot. There was nothing else to do.

Except wait for someone to find him.

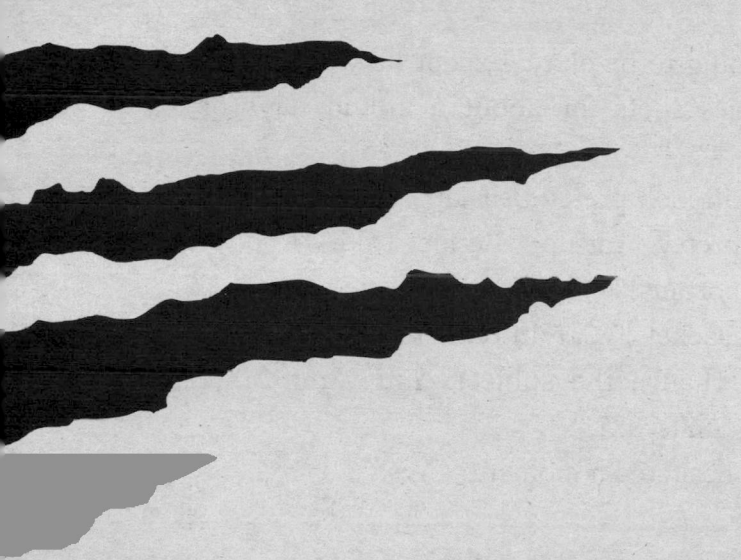

8

"I DON'T THINK WE NEED TO INVOLVE RILEY AND Raeburn," Calvin said.

They were in Calvin's tree house, which had become their unofficial hangout. About twenty feet off the ground, it was accessible by climbing up the tree and entering through a hinged opening in the floor. About the only thing Emmet didn't like about it was leaving Apollo on the ground. They hadn't yet figured out a way to safely get Apollo up there with them.

"Why not?" Emmet asked. "They're smart. And Raeburn knows a lot about bats. And by now I bet she's learned everything there is to know about hornets."

Emmet sat gingerly on one of the beanbags. He'd spent three days in the hospital, until doctors were sure he was going to be okay. Except he was going to need more rabies shots for about a zillion days or so, it seemed.

"You still look pretty beat-up," Calvin said.

"I am pretty beat-up," Emmet said. "I got attacked by bat-a-hornets!"

"Blood Jackets," Calvin replied.

"Don't change the subject. You want Dr. Catalyst stopped, don't you?"

Calvin hesitated a moment. "Yes."

"But?"

"I've known you for what? A few months now? You're not like other people. This guy is really dangerous. I get that you wanted to save your dad and Apollo and all, but you'll go charging after him. I have enough to do just trying to keep you from getting injured . . . or worse. I can't keep my eye on everyone."

Emmet knew this was partly true and partly false. Calvin was cool in a crisis — charging at a Pterogator or breaking into an abandoned amusement park. But the real reason he was protesting is that being around Riley made him nervous.

"Being around Riley makes you nervous," said Emmet.

"No, it doesn't!" Calvin protested.

"Yes, it does. And you're not responsible for everyone's safety. But, regardless, we need all hands on deck.

We don't need Riley and Raeburn to go anywhere dangerous, but we could use all the brains we can get. Besides, I think Riley and Raeburn can take care of themselves." Emmet shuddered, remembering a few weeks ago when they were attacked by the Muraecudas in the ocean, and how Raeburn used her snorkel like a weapon to get the giant beast to release its grip on Stuke. She was pretty fearless.

Calvin sighed. By now he must have learned it was useless to argue with Emmet.

"Do you ever wonder . . . ?" Calvin said.

"Yes. I wonder all the time. Can you be more specific?" Emmet asked.

"How Dr. Catalyst is always a step ahead of us? When he took your dad from the swamp, he had to know where your dad was going. I mean, what are the chances he'd just show up where your dad was? And at the beach with Stuke, he sets those things loose right where we were. And even when he took Apollo . . . I suppose he could have been waiting in the canal, but how did he know for sure you were even going to be home? It's like he always knows where we're going to be."

Emmet considered this a moment.

"Do you think he's having us followed?"

"Maybe," Calvin said. "But that would take a lot of planning and manpower. He'd need more than just himself."

"He has Dr. Newton. If Dr. Newton isn't really Dr. Catalyst, maybe he's an accomplice. And that's how he keeps track of us at school."

"I don't think so," Calvin said. "If the Newt is Dr. Catalyst, then he just took himself out of the equation. If he was keeping an eye on us, why would he pretend to be kidnapped?"

"He knew we were closing in. And so he faked another crime, like he faked his death in the Everglades. Which, I would like to point out, no one believed me about, and I turned out to be right. Again."

"Yeah, we know. But I still don't think he's following us," Calvin said. He stood up and started pacing.

"Why?"

"Because when we showed up in the swamp to rescue your dad, and at Undersea Land to save Apollo, he was surprised. We set off alarms, and he came running. But he didn't know we were coming. If he did, he would have just taken off or moved them to another location. We surprised him then, but he knew where we were those other times. Either he has someone on the inside, or . . ." Calvin let the words trail off.

"Bugs!" They both said at the same time.

"He's got listening or tracking devices planted, probably on our parents' cars, and at the NPS headquarters. Maybe even in our houses!" Emmet said.

Calvin nodded grimly.

"Could he have done that? Bugged the park head-quarters?" Emmet asked.

"It's a federal facility, and it has security and all that, but it's not like the CIA or the Pentagon. If you were determined enough, you could probably wire it for sound, at least. There isn't anything top secret going on there, so they don't have any reason to suspect that stuff. From what we've seen, he has the resources," Calvin said.

"So," Emmet said, smiling, momentarily forgetting about his painfully swollen face and his impending rabies shots. "This is how we're going to catch him!"

When their parents arrived at Calvin's house, they told them their theory.

9

THE NUMBER OF LOCATIONS DR. CATALYST COULD SAFELY operate from were rapidly dwindling. Now he took refuge in a long-abandoned motel along US Highway 1, south of Florida City. It was not ideal — he needed laboratory facilities — but it was on a deserted stretch of road, had power, and offered temporary shelter.

While pondering his next move, Dr. Catalyst poured over the calculations and simulation results for his next project. Part of his genius was his ability to turn his mind loose on several problems at once. So far, his calculations looked to be accurate.

On his tablet, he scrolled through his various Internet feeds. The idiot Newton was still sleeping on his cot. The man had nearly ruined everything. It had only been by luck that Dr. Catalyst stopped him before . . .

What was this? Dr. Catalyst expanded a window on his tablet. His feed to the NPS headquarters showed Dr. Geaux and Dr. Doyle examining the body of the Pterogator they had found in the park months ago. The discovery that had set all of these events in motion. What could they be looking for at this late date? He pulled up the audio.

"What are you looking for?" Dr. Geaux asked.

"It's . . . I'll know it when I find it," Dr. Doyle said as he removed a small tissue sample from the body. "As an abstract theory, it's understandable how he could recombine the DNA of alligators and birds — they're evolutionary relatives. Sharks, eels, and fish are also similar genetically, evolving from the same family. But bats and hornets? That's gene splicing and recombination at a level far beyond anything we've ever seen."

Dr. Catalyst laughed out loud as he watched. Of course it was. He was a genius, after all.

"Then I started thinking," Dr. Doyle said as he removed another sample from the corpse and placed it in a petri dish. "Once he created his first hybrid Pterogators, he cloned them to accelerate their numbers. Originally they all descended from a single 'copy.' But somehow, somewhere in the process, the Pterogators mutated and are now reproducing. There have been some new studies that suggest that all DNA carries the genetic coding for both male and female of a species. Way back when only bacteria existed on the planet, some biologists theorize that single-celled bacteria was absorbed by other bacteria. Eventually, evolution created males and females. But there is some evidence to suggest the base pairs for both sexes exist in certain chromosomes."

"I have no idea what you just said," Dr. Geaux joked.

Dr. Doyle laughed.

"My guess is a mutation in the gene sequence occurred somewhere. No species is ever static. People think evolution takes thousands, if not millions, of years, and it certainly can. But you can also see dramatic differences in some species in just a few generations. DNA is so complex. One little thing — the corruption of a single enzyme on a single chromosome — can set off a chain reaction. Then your clone is no longer a carbon copy of the original. Then it passes on those traits to the next clone, and if there's another corruption, it starts another cascade of changes within the genetic code."

"What a fool," Dr. Catalyst said out loud to the empty room. Although part of him wondered if the moron Doyle might have accidentally stumbled onto something. Hammer was his very first successful living hybrid. Nails had simply been a clone. And then he had cloned dozens more from there. The Pterogators should not have been able to reproduce. But they were. Something had happened. Even a scientist as inferior as Doyle the Dunce could luck into an explanation. Possibly.

"Are you thinking the amino acids?" Dr. Geaux asked.

"That's exactly what I'm thinking," Dr. Doyle answered. "That's where the building blocks of life begin. Just to gestate the eggs for these Pterogators you'd need numerous highly specialized chemicals and specific amino-acid transporters. If we can identify the unique components he used, we can look for where a person might have acquired the ingredients. It's not like you can pick up cloning supplies at a drugstore."

"And we can trace him that way, maybe find out who this loon is," Dr. Geaux said.

"Exactly. But we don't have the equipment we need here. I talked to a pathologist at the state crime lab in Miami. When we transfer the corpse there, we might be able to determine —"

"I already put the authorization through," Dr. Geaux said. "That is really good thinking, Ben. I knew asking you to come here was a good idea."

They stopped a moment to smile at each other. "I'm glad you did," Dr. Doyle said.

"Oh, good grief," Dr. Catalyst muttered as he watched the image on his screen.

Dr. Doyle took a body bag and unzipped it next to the dead Pterogator. Dr. Geaux helped him fit the creature inside and close it up.

"Let's get it in my truck," Dr. Doyle said. "The pathologist is going to meet me there. I've got to pick up Emmet, and then —"

"Why don't you go on? I'll get the boys and take them to my house. The sooner we can get this guy behind bars, the better. This might be the break we need."

"Are you sure you don't mind?" he asked.

"Not at all. Emmet is an absolute joy," she said.

Dr. Catalyst wanted to throw up. If by "joy," she meant an annoying, precocious little snot, then yes, Emmet Doyle was a *joy*. He watched as they hefted the creature off the table and left the room.

He stood up, rapidly pacing back and forth. Ever since the beginning, he'd wanted to recover the Pterogator corpse. It would give him valuable insight on his research, and perhaps allow him to discover why the creature had died. And what was happening to the Pterogators in the swamp.

If he moved quickly, he could intercept that fool Doyle and reclaim his property.

But there was something he would need to retrieve from one of his storage units first.

10

"DO YOU THINK HE BOUGHT IT?" EMMET ASKED.

"There's no reason to think he wouldn't," Dr. Geaux said. "He has no idea we discovered his surveillance. We had the FBI sweep the parking lots and outside the buildings. They didn't find anything aside from the camera in the lab and two audio feeds in the main office."

"He's just . . . Wouldn't he think it would be uncovered eventually? He's always thinking ahead," Emmet said.

Emmet considered himself the world's foremost Dr. Catalyst expert. From the time he and Calvin had rescued his father, Emmet understood Dr. Catalyst had an elaborate plan in place. Twice now they had stopped him, and yet he kept going, creating more creatures, endangering more people.

"It's possible. We're dealing with someone who is smart, crazy, and determined, and that's always a bad combination," she said.

They were driving in one of the task force SUVs along US 1 toward Miami. A few miles ahead, a member of the task force drove Dr. Doyle's truck. After Dr. Geaux and his dad had carried the Pterogator outside the lab, they switched up. An agent dressed in identical clothing to what his dad was wearing drove off in the truck, with a body bag stuffed full of rocks and newspapers in the back. The truck had four undercover cars trailing it, two in front, and a helicopter watching from high in the air. The state lab in Miami was also filled with agents and cops, ready for whatever might happen.

The SUV their group drove was a super-tricked-out law-enforcement vehicle. From their rear seats, Emmet and Calvin could watch the video feed from the helicopter on monitors that flipped down from the ceiling.

"Why would he care about getting back his Pterogator corpse enough to carjack my fake dad?" Emmet asked.

"We don't know that he will," Dr. Doyle answered. "But my guess has always been that we have his first viable Pterogator or one of his very early clones. I think, as a scientist, he's burning to get it back, and to know what happened to it. And if he thinks there's even the remotest possibility we could trace him through the amino-acid compounds he used, he'd try to prevent us from testing the corpse."

As head of the task force, Dr. Geaux was letting the professionals tail Dr. Doyle's truck. When Emmet heard about the plan, he insisted that he and Calvin be allowed to be there when Dr. Catalyst was arrested. Dr. Geaux, of course, refused. In the ensuing argument, Emmet had played every sympathy card he possessed, including pouting with his swollen face, until Dr. Geaux finally agreed. They would trail several miles behind the agent driving his dad's pickup, but once Dr. Catalyst was arrested, Emmet could have his moment. So he and Calvin sat in the back, glued to the monitors, while Dr. Doyle rode shotgun.

The screen showed his dad's truck driving along a stretch of road that was surrounded by swamp on both sides. *Even the ground in Florida is water*, Emmet thought. Or watery. Or a sponge. Whatever, he didn't like it. Ground should be solid.

A lot of police lingo came over the monitor as the officers and agents communicated with one another. The upshot of all the "Copy thats," and "10-4s," and "No suspect sighteds" was that so far no one had spotted anything suspicious.

Emmet couldn't stand the tension. Every time a voice

came over the radio, he leaned forward in the seat, staring at the monitor.

"Dude, you need to relax," Calvin said.

"I'll relax when he's enrolled at Convict College," Emmet said.

"Where?" Calvin asked.

Emmet shrugged. "Jail. I watched a prison documentary on TV the other night."

Calvin sighed.

The radio crackled with static, then a voice spoke up that Emmet recognized. It was Stuke's dad. He was a Florida City cop and had joined the task force after Stuke was attacked by the Muraecudas. He was probably the one person who wanted Dr. Catalyst caught as much as Emmet did.

"Unit one, I've got eyes on a gray, late-model Pontiac sedan. It's been following the truck for the past six miles, over."

"Copy that, unit two. Can you ID a driver?"

"Negative, unit one, tinted windows," Stuke's dad answered. "Bring up unit three to my position, I'm pulling off at the next exit, then I'll move to the back of the line. Keep rotating. Everyone stay calm. If it is him, we don't want to spook him. Chopper one, do you have him?"

"Copy that, unit two," the pilot answered.

The camera from the helicopter pulled back, and they could now see the tiny image of the pickup driving down the road. About a quarter of a mile behind it was the gray sedan. Emmet couldn't tell which of the other vehicles was being driven by the undercover cops.

He sat up even straighter in the seat now, as did Calvin. There was tense, unbearable silence on the radio for several seconds.

"Unit one, this is unit three. Sedan is accelerating. It's closing on the truck."

Emmet clinched his fists.

"Unit one, this is chopper one. It's two car lengths back. Unit three, move to intercept." Emmet marveled at how calm they remained on the radio.

"Negative, unit three, negative. They could be passing. Hold . . ."

"All units! All units! This is unit three, gray sedan just rammed the truck. All units converge! All units conver — Whoa!"

Emmet watched everything unfold like it was in slow motion. The gray sedan shot forward and rammed the rear end of the pickup. The driver of the pickup fought for control, swerving slightly to the right. At that point, the gray sedan pulled out and sped forward alongside the truck, turning in an attempt to push the pickup off the road. But the truck hit the brakes just enough so that the sedan traveled too far forward and was now being pushed along by the pickup.

The gray car turned sideways, its tires digging into the pavement, and it suddenly flipped several times, riding up along the guardrail at the side of the road and then tumbling over it into the swamp.

"What just happened?!" Emmet cried.

"I don't know," Dr. Geaux said. She grabbed the microphone on the radio and started talking into it really fast.

"We've got the sedan! All units, there has been a collision, repeat, the sedan has gone over the embankment into the water," Lieutenant Stukaczowski said over the radio. "Get EMS and paramedics out here! All units respond, code three!"

Dr. Geaux hit the lights and sirens on the SUV and accelerated into the passing lane. A few miles later, a long line of cars was stopped in the road. Ahead of them, the light bars of numerous emergency vehicles flashed over the accident scene. Dr. Geaux steered their vehicle onto the shoulder, blowing past the backed-up traffic. When they arrived, the pickup truck was crunched against the guardrail, its right side dented up pretty badly, but the driver was standing beside it and appeared to be okay.

"All of you stay inside this car," Dr. Geaux said,

slowing the SUV and slamming it in park. She opened the door and rushed toward the scene.

They watched the flurry of activity for several minutes. There was constant chatter over the radio. On the monitor they could see Stuke's dad and several other law-enforcement agents gesturing and waving their arms. Two men pulled rifles from their vehicles and stationed themselves next to the road where the gray sedan had gone into the swamp.

"Why do those guys have rifles?" Emmet asked. "We want him alive!"

"Gators," Calvin said. "If they send somebody into the water to go after the car's driver, there could be gators nearby. If they come after the rescuers, then those officers will shoot them."

"Remind me never to learn to drive as long as I live in Florida," Emmet said.

Two police officers waded into the swamp. The gray sedan had gone in rear-end-first, but the chopper was too high to see everything clearly. Emmet looked out the window to see a tow truck pulling up in front of them, blocking their view.

Emmet put his hand on the door handle.

"Don't even think about it," his dad said from the front seat.

"But — !" Emmet protested.

"Not a chance," Dr. Doyle said.

They waited. The radio was silent. Finally, Dr. Geaux appeared, coming around the side of the tow truck and walking toward the SUV. She did not look happy as she opened the door and climbed back in the driver's seat.

"Who was it? Did you find him? Is he alive?" Emmet started peppering her with questions, but stopped when Dr. Geaux pounded her hands on the steering wheel in frustration.

"It was no one. He played us. The car was empty. He had a remote operating system driving the car. He must have suspected all along that we were trying to set him up."

"How did he know?" Emmet said, barely able to conceal his disappointment.

"I wish I knew, Emmet," she said. "I wish I knew."

The line of stopped cars behind them grew longer and longer. The police finally shut down the highway and allowed drivers to turn around in the median and travel in the opposite direction. Amidst all the confusion and chaos, no one noticed the late-model pickup that followed suit, bouncing slowly across the grass between the divided highway, and then onto the road heading back toward Florida City.

Where it sped quickly away.

11

THE NEXT DAY, EMMET WAS IN A SOMBER MOOD. HE couldn't concentrate on his classes. The thought that Dr. Catalyst outsmarted them was hard to accept. He even frowned through lunch, which was normally his favorite part of the day.

"Why are you frowning so much?" Stuke asked. Good old Stuke. Never afraid of asking the tough questions.

"I just can't believe he beat us," Emmet said.

Nobody said anything. Stuke was still limping around but had given up the walker. Emmet's face had healed to the point where he at least no longer looked like an extra in a horror movie. At first he'd been worried kids would make fun of him, but the Blood Jackets were attacking people all over Florida City. The fact that he was the first — and survived — gave him a little street cred.

To make matters worse, Emmet's dad and Calvin's mom had teamed up on them, and "highly encouraged" they join the Tasker Middle School Service Club. It was something the new principal had started. They had to stay after school and take part in service projects, like helping out at concerts, basketball games, and other school events. Calvin agreed without protest. Emmet immediately understood it was an attempt to keep him from sticking his nose in Dr. Catalyst Business.

"Do we really have to do this Service Club thing tonight?" he asked Calvin.

"Yes," Calvin said. "What choice do we have?"

"We don't do it, go hide in the tree house, and tell our parents we did it anyway," Emmet said.

"Dude!" Calvin said in alarm. "That would be lying."

"Not if we told them something else came up," Emmet said.

"Like what?" Calvin huffed.

"Finding you-know-who," Emmet said.

"No. We have to do it," Calvin said.

"But why?" Emmet whined.

"Because you're in the club now," Calvin said.

"Do I have to wear the outfit?" Emmet said. "A white shirt and black pants? Why don't you just hang a Kick

Me sign on my back?" The new principal had also decided that the Service Club members were required to wear dorky outfits.

"Don't worry, Emmet," Riley said. "Raeburn and I signed up, too. Misery loves company, or something like that."

"Great . . ." Emmet stalled his rant, because Stuke was staring off at something at the far end of the cafeteria. "Stuke . . . what are you looking at?"

"Huh? Oh, nuthin'," Stuke answered. "Just wonder what that gross stuff is, leaking out of the vent up there on the wall."

"What gross stuff?" Emmet turned around and looked across the cafeteria. Sure enough, something icky was leaking out of it. A thin streak of grayish-white gunk was running down the wall beneath the vent.

"Okay, that *is* gross," Emmet said. "Wonder what it is?"

"Don't know," Stuke said. "Never saw it before."

"Maybe it's where they keep the lasagna," Emmet said. Riley and Raeburn chuckled. Calvin raised his eyebrows, which was the equivalent of a belly laugh for him.

Stuke shook his head. "I'm pretty sure they keep the lasagna in the freezer." He was still on painkillers after his encounter with the Muraecuda.

"Riiighht," Emmet said. The bell rang, and they all stood and emptied their trays as they headed off to classes. The mysterious stain was forgotten.

The rest of the day, Emmet paid very little attention to schoolwork. His mind wandered, thinking about the previous day's events over and over. He wondered if they had given something away or tipped off Dr. Catalyst somehow. No matter how hard he thought about it, he couldn't figure it out. He finally concluded that the crazy environmentalist had just been extremely cautious. And lucky.

Emmet and Calvin stayed after school, helping get everything set up for the concert. Their first job was pulling out a bunch of long carts with folding chairs stacked on them from beneath the bleachers in the gym.

Emmet was handing over the chairs while Calvin set them up, when a big glop of something white and gray splattered on the floor next to them. They looked up to find it had fallen from a vent in the ceiling.

And it smelled. It smelled really bad.

"Ugh. Could that be any grosser?" Emmet said, backing away from it. "What the heck is it?"

"I'm guessing bird poop," Calvin said.

"It looks like the same stuff from the lunchroom. And it stinks! Ewww," Emmet said, putting more distance between himself and the pile of glop.

"A bird is probably stuck in one of the vents. It happens sometimes," Calvin said. "We should probably clean it up."

"*You* should probably clean it up," Emmet declared. "In case you've forgotten, I'm still recovering from a horrible medical trauma. You wouldn't want me to get an infection, would you?"

"You won't . . . That's not . . ." Calvin sighed, knowing he wasn't going to win the argument, and left to get something to clean up the mess. Emmet resumed pulling chairs off the cart and setting them up in rows.

As he worked, he was unaware that in the ventilation system above him, the colony was coming awake.

Soon it would be time to feed.

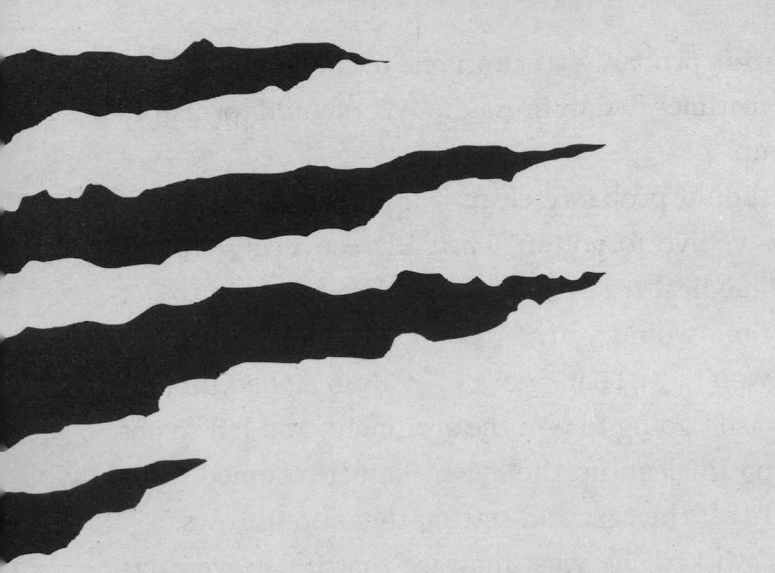

12

DR. NEWTON WOKE UP WITH A START. HE HAD BEEN dreaming, and he sat up on the edge of the cot trying to recall the details, but they faded away quickly. It was something to do with being locked away in a deserted . . . He looked around. It was not a dream. It was reality.

He had completely lost track of how many days he'd been locked away here. A week? Two weeks? He desperately needed a shower. Something had gone horribly wrong with the plan. If he had been missing for so long, someone should have been looking for him.

Of course, he had no idea where he was. For all he knew, he could have been put on a plane and flown to another country. He doubted it, but it was a possibility.

Still, this heat felt like Florida. There was the familiar tackiness of the humidity, so thick it made you feel like water was literally hanging in the air and would stick to your skin whenever you moved. Florida: The only state where you could sweat while taking a shower.

He stood and stalked about the cell. His handcuffed wrist and the chain attached to it allowed him to reach the water cooler, toilet, and box of food, but not the door. No matter how he stretched, it was just out of reach. Whoever locked him in here took no chance on him finding a way to pick or break the lock.

As he paced, he suddenly realized the handcuff was looser on his wrist. Days of captivity had caused him to lose some weight. Twisting his arm slightly, he found the manacle had a bit more give than before. Perhaps there was enough space now to work his hand free! Glancing up at the camera — knowing it was watching his every move — he lay back down on the cot and threw his arm over his eyes, as he if he were attempting to sleep. Tossing and turning, he finally flipped over on one side, with his back to the camera.

Very slowly, he worked the handcuff over his hand. There was a trick to freeing oneself from handcuffs this way. The method was to use your shoulder and arm muscles to manipulate your wrist. Twisting your hand and wrist muscles just caused the tissues to swell, making it more difficult to get free.

It was a painful trick. The cuff scraped and dug at his skin until it bled. It took enormous concentration to keep the rest of his body still, while he slowly maneuvered his shoulder and arm. Thankfully, whatever sleepy drugs were in the water helped dull the pain.

Finally, the cuff slipped from Dr. Newton's hand.

He was free! He showed no reaction. Hoping whoever was monitoring him would believe he was sleeping restlessly.

He pushed the ratcheted point of the cuff through the loop, until the pointed end stuck out the other side. Using it as a lever, he pried at the chain, pulling one of the links far enough apart that he was able to work the handcuff completely free from the chain.

Now he had to pause and think. There was no question that he was being watched. If he tried to pick the lock on the door, or pry his way out, someone could arrive and stop him before he escaped. But if he waited until dark, he might have a better chance. It was unlikely he was being observed around the clock.

The hours went by slowly, and the wait was excruciating, but eventually the interior of the warehouse grew dimmer. Still he waited.

Finally, it was as dark as it was going to get.

He stood up and hurried to the door. With his hands, he felt around the latch and lock, looking for any weak spot where he might be able to pry it loose. Finding nothing, he used the thick handcuff as a bludgeon and pounded away. Again and again he struck at it, his frustration growing with every blow. It took a long time and he had to stop and rest his arm several times.

On his next swing he heard a crack.

The housing had separated ever so slightly from the metal door. His arm was nearly worn out, but he reached through the bars and struck the lock several more times, until there was enough room to work the pointed end of the handcuff into the crack. He wiggled and worked with his primitive tool, prying the lock completely loose. Finally, with a resounding *pop*, the lock came free and the door swung open.

Dr. Newton gathered up some protein bars from the box of food and stuffed them in his pockets. He walked through the cell door, half expecting alarms to sound, but was met only with silence.

He scurried across the floor of the warehouse to the exterior door. To his joy, he found it unlocked. This was good and bad news. Whoever had taken him never expected him to escape. But it also told him he was someplace very remote, with very little chance of being accidentally discovered. There was most likely a long, arduous hike ahead of him to reach civilization.

Dr. Newton didn't care. He was free.

He opened the door and ran off into the night.

A small black box was built into the wall near the door, on the front of which glowed a small green light.

As Dr. Newton passed through the door, the light changed from green to blinking red.

13

EMMET SAT ON THE BLEACHERS NEXT TO CALVIN, RILEY, and Raeburn, all of them in their white shirts with black pants, watching the Tasker Middle School band concert.

The "music" was nearly unbearable. Emmet was all for extracurricular activities, and he supported the idea of the band in theory. So long as he didn't have to attend the concerts, or hear the music, or wear the clothes. He had to figure out a way to drop out of the Service Club. He was never going to catch Dr. Catalyst if he spent all his extra time cleaning up after concerts.

While they waited for the program to end, Emmet compiled a list of things he would rather do than go to a middle-school band concert. He was deciding between walking barefoot across broken glass or having a double root canal when there was a loud crash from the ceiling vent directly over where most of the crowd was sitting in the rows of folding chairs.

Emmet looked up just in time to see the metal grate fall to the gym floor with a resounding crash. It just narrowly missed giving the mother of a fifth-grade trombone player a solid conk on the head.

At first, there was silence. Even the band had stopped playing, a few straggling notes echoing throughout the gymnasium. Everyone stared at the open space in the ceiling in silence. The entire gym quieted, but no one could take their eyes off the gaping hole.

Then a writhing swarm of Blood Jackets poured out of the opening in the ceiling. The creatures came in wave after wave, dipping and darting everywhere. Their cries alternated between the chittering bat noise and the hum of an angry hornet. And, as always, there was the sound of the flapping leathery wings. It seemed like it was the sounds that drove the people mad. As if some primitive instinct in the brain compelled them to escape upon hearing the dreadful noise. The sound meant danger. Death. Run away from the sound. Chaos erupted in the gym as everyone in attendance rose as one, rushing toward the door.

"What the — ?" Raeburn said.

"Get out!" Emmet shouted. "Find a door! Get out!"

The four of them dashed down the bleachers to the gymnasium floor, but it was a turbulent mass of confusion. Parents grabbed children and ran. The creatures hovered over their heads. The more everyone ran and screamed, the more feverish the flying monsters became.

Riley was knocked to the ground by a kid holding a snare drum over his head; Calvin helped her scramble to her feet. More Blood Jackets flooded out of the vent in the ceiling and raised the shouting and trampling to higher levels.

"This way!" Emmet shouted. The other three followed him toward the wall of the gym. A single Blood Jacket swooped down at Calvin, and its claws raked his head. Calvin waved his hands and arms, trying to scare the creature off, but nothing worked. He dropped to his knees and was about to cover up, when something whirred through the air and connected with the animal, sending it careering into the wall. It fell to the floor, flapping its wings, disoriented and wobbling around.

Riley had picked up one of the metal music stands and swung it like a baseball bat, hitting the flying creature flush. Another swooped down and she delivered another wallop, sending the winged monster swirling away with an agonizing cry. Another creature took up the attack and suffered the same fate. Riley was playing a game of airborne Whac-A-Mole. And winning. At least for the moment.

"Awesome," Emmet said, picking up his own music stand. Calvin and Raeburn followed suit.

The main doors leading out to the hallway and the exits from the building were clogged with people desperate to flee. The Blood Jackets were everywhere, soaring over the crowd. The entire scene was right out of the scariest horror movie they had ever seen.

Raeburn swung her music stand and drove one of the creatures back. "We have to get across the gym to the other doors!" she said.

"No way, it's too far, those things will overwhelm us!" Emmet cried.

"Over here!" he heard Calvin shout.

Calvin gestured to them from beneath the bleachers. Like in most school gyms, the bleachers at Tasker Middle School were collapsible, folding into the wall when there were no activities taking place. Calvin led them underneath the wooden seats, where they found some temporary relief in the partially enclosed space. A few of the creatures tried to fly in after them, but the close quarters inhibited their ability to maneuver. They flew away in search of easier targets.

The crowd was nearly trampling one another to get away. Parents shouted for their children, their voices drowned out in a cacophony of names. The relentless attacks from the Blood Jackets and the bottleneck at the doors had frozen everyone in place. The flying pests reminded Emmet of a school of fish swimming in the ocean. They came in groups almost like they were flying in formation. And when some instinct they possessed identified a target, they descended in unison, attacking without mercy.

"Where did they come from?" Emmet said.

"The vent," Calvin replied.

"I know *the vent*! I mean how did they get inside the school?" Emmet said.

"Maybe Dr. Catalyst?" Raeburn offered.

"Maybe. We've got to help those people," Emmet said.

"How?" Riley said.

Emmet looked around. A few feet from the end of the bleachers, he spied a fire alarm on the wall.

"Calvin, call 9-1-1," he said.

Calvin reached for his pocket but stopped midway with a sheepish expression. "I put my phone in my backpack when we changed clothes," he said.

"Ah, heck. Me too. I left it on the bleachers," Emmet said. "We've got to do something. Everybody stay here."

"What are — ?" Calvin started to speak, but Emmet took off running from his spot.

Once clear of the bleachers, he held the music stand over his head and raced toward the nearby wall. Blood Jackets dived at him, crashing into the stand's metal tray. Emmet staggered to the wall, found the red fire alarm, and pulled the handle.

The noise was deafening. A high-pitched klaxon alarm, complete with flashing strobe lights, pulsated through the room. The noise had an immediate impact on the creatures. They screeched and flew up toward the ceiling, looking for a way out of the room.

The momentary halt in the attack allowed some of the crowd to finally make their way through the door from the gym into the hallway. Emmet scampered back under the cover of the bleachers. The brain-rattling noise of the alarm continued.

"What are we going to do? We can't stay under here!" Raeburn shouted.

"We need to wait a minute! Let the crowd thin out, then we'll make a run for it!" Emmet said.

The Blood Jackets flew around and around, circling the gym like a living cyclone. After a moment, they descended on those remaining in the gym still trying to jam through the door.

Three of them came zooming under the bleachers. Calvin and Riley batted them away with their stands.

"They're attacking again!" Calvin shouted. "It's too jammed up! We'll never make it out!"

"Well, I'd love to hear another plan!" Emmet yelled back. "If we try running across the gym to the other door, they'll be all over us!"

"Over there. The closet where they keep all the athletic equipment," Calvin said, pointing.

In the space behind the bleachers, tucked into a corner of the gym, was a small alcove. It held a closet with double steel doors. All the stuff the PE teachers used in gym class was stored inside.

"It's probably locked!" Raeburn said.

"Probably!" Calvin agreed.

Before anyone could say anything, Calvin darted out from under the bleachers and sprinted to the door. He swung the music stand like an axe and knocked the doorknob off the door. The door popped open.

"Hurry!" he said.

The three of them sprinted after him and into the closet. Calvin pulled the door shut.

"Oh wow, oh wow, oh wow," Emmet said.

They listened to the chaos on the other side of the door. The shrieking alarm, the now receding screams of the crowd, and the chittering of the Blood Jackets was muffled through the door. Calvin found the light switch and flipped it on.

They listened intently as the noise went on for several more minutes. Finally, the screams ended and all they could hear was the fire alarm . . . and the screeching of the flying beasts. For a moment they didn't know whether to be relieved or terrified. They had a temporary reprieve, but part of them knew the vicious beasts would soon find their way inside their momentary sanctuary. Their skin tingled with fear, and all of them, even Calvin, were feeling jumpy. They tried not to think about what was happening to the people outside the room.

"What are we going to do?" Riley asked.

"I vote we stay here until help arrives," Emmet said.

"Sounds like a plan," Racburn said.

Suddenly, a familiar rustling, chittering noise sounded from above their heads. Could it be? Had the Blood Jackets tracked them through the ventilation system so quickly?

"No way! You've got to be kidding me! How did they find us?" Emmet said.

"We're going to have to run for it now," Riley said.

"No! We'll be okay in here if we block up that vent," Emmet said. "There are hundreds of those things out there. They'll eat us alive!"

"We can't stay here," Riley said, watching the vent cover creaking and bending with each blow from the Blood Jackets.

Calvin had been digging around in the piles of equipment at the back of the closet. He stood up now, not quite smiling, but not *not* smiling.

"These might help," he said.

He held a football helmet in each hand.

14

DR. CATALYST WOKE TO A RAPID BEEPING COMING FROM his tablet computer. One of his proximity alarms had been tripped. Running his fingers over the glass, he discovered it was for the facility where he had been forced to take the dunce Newton. The door alarm had been activated.

He checked his cameras before taking an unnecessary trip. Sometimes a door blew open in the wind, and even the best alarms occasionally malfunctioned.

The interior of the building appeared on his screen. The door to the facility was standing wide open. It still could have been caused by the wind.

But when he switched to a view of the cell, he let out

a loud curse. That door was also open. The cell was empty. Somehow, the idiot Newton had escaped.

"How is that possible?" he muttered to himself.

The facility was remote, and only accessible by boat. It would take him at least an hour to get there. Maybe more. For a moment Dr. Catalyst wondered if he should even bother. Newton had failed miserably. Now the fool would likely die in the swamp. It might not be the worst thing in the world to just let him go.

But he couldn't be sure.

Dr. Catalyst sighed.

"First the Doyle brat and now this loser," he muttered. As he gathered up equipment — water and some other supplies — he cursed those who vexed him so, interfering with his plans.

He pulled his pistol from the holster, checking to make sure it was loaded.

As he held the gun out in front of him, sighting down the barrel, a thought flitted through his brain: Perhaps, if he did recover Newton, he would carry him deep into the swamp. And get rid of him. Dr. Catalyst was rapidly losing patience with those who hindered his efforts.

As he picked up his truck keys, his tablet beeped again with a news-broadcast alert. He clicked on the link and a window opened showing a live feed from one of the local TV stations. A breathless blond reporter stood outside a school building surrounded by dozens of police cars and fire trucks, their lights blinking.

"Details are still forthcoming," she said. "What we do know is that tonight's performance of the Tasker Middle School concert band was interrupted by the appearance of hundreds of the new hybrid creatures created by Dr. Catalyst. These Blood Jackets appear to be a combination of vampire bats and hornets. Whatever their genetic makeup, they are extremely aggressive, and are responsible for dozens of injuries in and around Florida City in the last few days."

Dr. Catalyst smiled. The news was rapidly improving his mood.

"Reports from witnesses say that the creatures entered the gymnasium through a ventilation duct. There, they attacked the attendees, injuring dozens of innocent concertgoers. Ambulances and paramedics are on the scene, and the building has been sealed. It is unknown at this time how many of the creatures — or people — are still inside the building. But authorities have told me that they will keep all doors closed to prevent these Blood Jackets from escaping and causing further injury. Jim, I'm sending it back to you in the studio."

The screen changed to a talking head in a dark suit with hair that looked as if it had been shellacked in place. He started blathering on about Dr. Catalyst and his attacks on the citizens of South Florida and blah, blah, blah.

Dr. Catalyst closed the link. The transmitters he'd placed on the creatures had not worked as well as he hoped, giving him trouble in tracking the colonies. Trying to find where the hybrids were nesting proved a daunting task. Their ability to fly allowed them to cover much more territory than the Pterogators. But the transmitter had to be tiny to not interfere with their flight capabilities. Their range was extremely limited. Now he knew where at least one of the colonies was nesting.

Newton would have to wait.

He could not pass up the opportunity to see his magnificent creations in action. He was certain the police, or animal control, or some of Dr. Geaux's toadies would attempt to destroy the nest at the middle school. And they might even succeed.

But right now, his very own invasive species was wreaking vengeance in Florida City.

This was something not to be missed.

15

"**P**LEASE TELL ME YOU'RE NOT SUGGESTING A GAME OF football right now!" Emmet shouted over the noise of the fire alarm.

"No. Put these on!" Calvin tossed the helmets to Riley and Raeburn. Then he pulled another from the cupboard and tossed it to Emmet before donning his own.

The Blood Jackets were screeching and throwing themselves against the vent. The cover was composed of thin sheet metal slats with screws holding it in place. It looked to Emmet like it was going to give way any minute.

"Here!" Calvin said. Next to the cupboard of helmets were bags of shoulder pads, shin guards, and everything one needed to suit up for a game of football. In the corner of the closet was a plastic barrel full of field hockey sticks. Everyone put on pads and Calvin handed out sticks to each of them. They were lighter and easier to handle than the music stands, at least.

"What now?" Riley said.

"Check the gym!" Calvin shouted.

Emmet cracked open the door and was rewarded with a dozen of the creatures immediately trying to claw their way through the tiny crack.

He screamed and slammed the door.

"What's the situation?" Calvin asked.

"It's a little south of not good!" Emmet said. "Those things are all over the place. And they seem hungry!" He looked up at the vent. One of the furry little monsters was trying to wiggle its way through one of the bent slats. They were relentless.

"Pretty soon they're going to be all over us," Raeburn said.

"Okay," Calvin said. "On the count of three, we open the door and make a break for it. The helmets and pads will give us some protection, and the hockey sticks will do the rest."

"Are you sure?" Emmet said.

"No," Calvin replied.

"Did you ever notice you always attack monsters

with sticks? You need to start carrying a bazooka in that backpack of yours," Emmet complained.

"Get ready to run," Calvin said, ignoring him. "One. Two. Three!"

He charged forward and threw back the closet door. It was like he had opened up a can of chaos. The Blood Jackets were on them even before they could clear the doorway. The appearance of their colony members drove the creatures in the vent berserk, and they finally pushed through, sending the cover clattering to the floor. The closet was instantly filled with a black screeching cloud.

"Don't stop to look! Run!" Emmet shouted over the still-earsplitting alarm. For a moment he cursed himself for pulling it.

They struggled to make their way toward the gym doors, but it was like trying to walk against the onrushing wind of a tornado. The concertgoers had managed to escape into the hallways, leaving hundreds of the monsters circling in the air of the open gym, frantic with hunger. When the cries of their colony mates alerted them to the presence of new warm-blooded creatures in their midst, they dove upon the four padded humans with a blood lust.

"Keep moving!" Emmet shouted encouragement. He swung the hockey stick in a wide swath. It connected with several of the creatures, knocking them to the ground. The air was so thick with wings and fur and antennae, it was nearly impossible not to hit several of them with a single swing.

"We can't go this way!" Calvin said. "There's too many of them!"

Emmet looked back at the closet, but the creatures were still pouring out of the ventilation duct. Maybe they could get back in the closet and close up the vent somehow, but if that didn't work they would be trapped in an enclosed space with a zillion Blood Jackets and nowhere to hide.

"Under the bleachers!" Emmet said.

They dashed back to the bleachers and moved beneath them along the wall. They couldn't swing their sticks in the enclosed space, but the Blood Jackets were limited as well. Crouching, they ran along the back wall to the other end of the gym. The flying monsters followed, throwing themselves at the bleachers and heaving through the openings.

One of them flew right at Emmet's head and latched onto the face mask, clawing at him through the small openings and giving Emmet the opportunity to see its beady eyes, large fangs, and spindly wings up close. He shook the helmet from side to side, trying to throw the beast off it, but it held tight.

"Get off!" he yelled. "Get off!"

Riley reached out with her stick and flicked the bat to the side.

"Thanks!" Emmet said.

They arrived at the other end of the bleachers and paused. The Blood Jackets hovered and darted in the air, trying to reach them beneath the bleachers, waiting for them to leave their sheltered spot. One step out and they would be covered in the tiny beasts.

"I really hate this plan," Emmet said.

"We've got to use the hallway to get out of here," Calvin said.

There was a set of doors about thirty feet away. To Emmet it seemed like thirty miles. Calvin was right. The exits leading outside were on the other side of the gymnasium. They'd never make it crossing the open floor. The hall doors were their only option.

He traced their route in his mind. Through the double doors into the hallway, turn right for about twenty yards and then left past the office. Then keep running until they reached the main doors.

"Let's do it," Raeburn said.

She sprinted for the doors.

Emmet, Calvin, and Riley followed her.

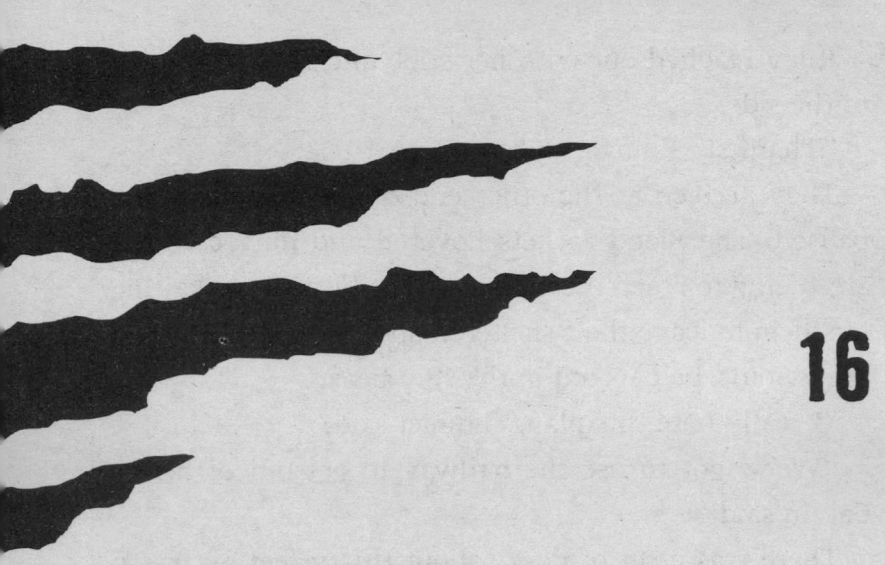

16

DR. CATALYST PULLED INTO THE TASKER MIDDLE SCHOOL parking lot. The darkened sky was awash with the flashing lights of emergency vehicles. Before leaving his hotel room, he'd grabbed a black Windbreaker with FBI written across the back, and threw it on. He always kept several sets of fake identities and uniforms handy, including authentic-looking credentials. Driving through the city streets, he parked the truck at the emergency perimeter set up around Tasker Middle School. Approaching the barricade and keeping his damaged right arm in his pocket, he flashed his credentials to the policeman who was manning the barricade and speaking into a two-way. His name tag said STUKACZOWSKI.

"My name is Agent Winchester, out of the Miami office," Dr. Catalyst said. "I heard your alert as I was driving back to the city. Thought I'd stop and see if there was something I could do to help."

Lieutenant Stukaczowski looked hard at the badge and then up at Dr. Catalyst.

"We've got a situation here. Have you heard about that Dr. Catalyst creep?"

Dr. Catalyst tried hard not to smile. "Only what I read in the papers and hear around the office. I usually work on cyber-crime cases."

"Yeah, well, he's a real nutcase. He's got some kind of genetically altered bats he's let loose now, and some of them have gotten inside the school. There was a band concert tonight and a lot of the critters went after the kids and their parents. It's chaos. Thirty people injured so far," Lieutenant Stukaczowski said.

"What a madman," Dr. Catalyst said.

"Don't need to tell me twice," Stukaczowski said.

"Do you need an extra hand?"

"Honestly, no. I think we've got it covered."

Dr. Catalyst was about to ask him another question when he saw a silver Buick he recognized pull up about twenty yards away.

"All right, then," he said. "I'll be going. Good luck."

He hurried back to his truck, making sure Dr. Geaux did not see him as she exited the car. If she did, everything would be over. Climbing back into the vehicle, he sat with his head down and his cell phone placed by his ear, as if he were taking a call. His window was rolled down, and he could hear Dr. Geaux and Dr. Doyle as they ran to Lieutenant Stukaczowski.

"What's the situation, Tom?" she asked.

"Those bat things got into the school during the concert. Bunch of people got bitten up and stung pretty bad. Some have already been taken to the hospital. We think we —"

"Have you seen Emmet and Calvin?" she asked.

"What?" Stukaczowski shook his head. "No. Why?"

"There were at the concert tonight," Dr. Doyle said.

"Well that doesn't mean —" said Lieutenant Stukaczowski.

"Is *everybody out*?" Dr. Geaux shouted.

"We think so. . . . We don't know for sure."

"We've got to go check." She started to push through the barricade.

"Rosalita," Stukaczowski said, taking her by the arm. "We can't go in. We open one of those doors and we'll have hundreds of those things loose and more people will get injured. The firefighters are trying to figure out a way to get inside safely. Let me call it in."

As Dr. Catalyst watched from his vehicle, Lieutenant Stukaczowski keyed the two-way. "All units this is

Command One. I need visual confirmation on students Calvin Geaux and Emmet Doyle. Check all ER units. Get eyes on them, people." A series of "copy thats" came back over Lieutenant Stukaczowski's radio.

Dr. Catalyst backed up his truck and pulled away, slowly circling the school. The streets around the building were full of emergency vehicles. If any of the Blood Jackets were around, he didn't see them. The colony likely had an entrance and exit into the school by which they departed each night. By now they had probably found a nearby hunting ground where they gathered the necessary amounts of blood. Something must have happened to cause the attack inside the school, perhaps some threat to their nest. He had chosen the baldfaced hornet specifically for this reason. They were fierce protectors of their homes.

But if what he had heard was true, if that sanctimonious little brat Emmet Doyle was still inside . . . well, this could be an opportunity that might not present itself again.

Circling the school, he discovered that most of the police, fire, and rescue efforts were concentrated at the front. It made sense. Most of the victims inside would instinctively rush toward the front door in their attempts to get to safety. That is where the first responders would concentrate their resources. But the back of the school was relatively free of any activity. None of the emergency personnel were thinking that someone might try to get into the school, only to get out.

Dr. Catalyst turned down a side street and parked his truck at the curb. From the truck's toolbox mounted behind the cab, he removed a black ski mask and several dozen long plastic zip ties. He was still wearing his FBI Windbreaker. Anyone who spotted him would likely assume he was part of the rescue effort.

Hurrying down the street, he cut across the rear parking lot to an emergency-exit door hidden in an alcove along the back wall. He could hear the fire alarm blaring inside the building. That would cover his entrance. The door was locked, but with the handle of his pistol he knocked out one of the door's glass panes. Reaching through, he pulled on the bar and the door popped open.

Before he entered the school, he sifted through his pocket and pulled out a small electronic device, roughly the size of a smartphone, and switched it on. The device was his own invention, a high-frequency transmitter that was designed to disrupt the bats' echolocation ability, making them think he was an undesirable food source. If it worked, it would prevent his being swarmed by the creatures. He'd carried it with him ever since releasing them.

Once inside, Dr. Catalyst listened for the sound of voices over the shrieking fire alarm but heard nothing. He quickly hustled down the hallway to the next door and looped a zip tie through the handles, securing it. Someone would have to cut through it from the inside before they could get away. The thought of it made him smile. He would work his way around the entire building, securing all the doors, making sure no one could get in or out.

If Emmet and Calvin *were* still inside, they would be trapped until his Blood Jackets finished them off.

The very thought of it made Dr. Catalyst absolutely gleeful.

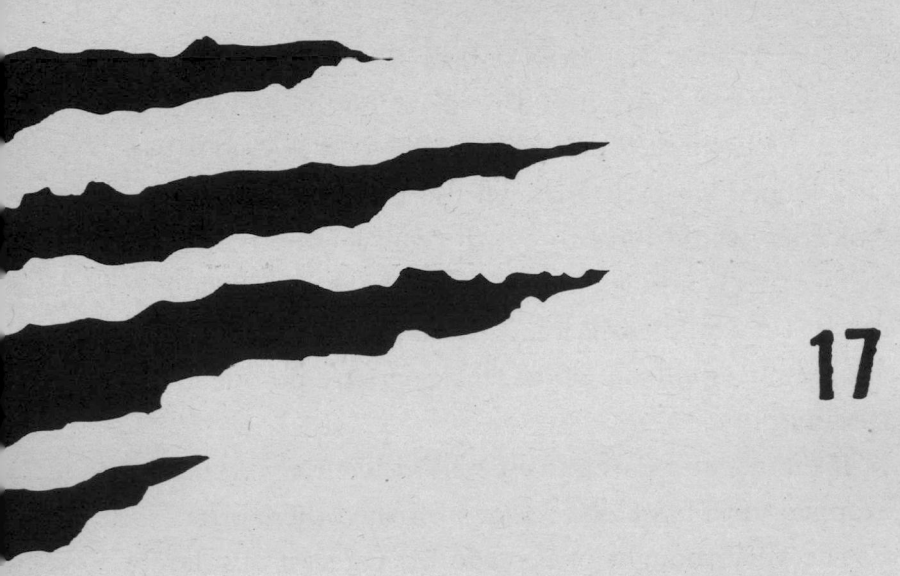

17

DR. NEWTON WASN'T SURE HOW LONG HE'D BEEN FREE. A couple of hours, at least. It was now completely dark and he was wishing with all his heart that Dr. Catalyst had invented a genetically altered super-creature that preyed on mosquitoes. As he trudged through the swamp, with only the moonlight to guide him, he had become a walking all-you-can-eat buffet.

He was taking a route to the southeast. One he hoped would return him to some form of civilization before long. After leaving the warehouse, he had headed straight north, going deeper into the swamp. This had been done intentionally. He hoped his captor would assume he'd head immediately to the south, toward the ocean. Moving north would increase his chances of getting away. Now, as the mosquitoes surrounded him in a cloud, he began to regret his decision.

He turned east for a while, and then southeast, which should theoretically lead him to a town, or at least a stream or river he could follow to one. If nothing else, he would reach the ocean eventually. Right now, he'd even settle for stumbling across a deserted fishing camp.

The mosquitoes were relentless. Weakly, he knelt beside a small bog and rubbed mud into his face and arms. It would hopefully provide some level of protection from the maddening insects until it dried and flaked off. As he stood, something shrieked in the forest about thirty or forty yards behind him. He could hear the rattling of the branches and leaves as a very large animal wended through the canopy of trees. Moving in his direction. Dr. Newton stopped and stared through the foliage but couldn't see anything.

It was probably a nervous eagle, or an osprey, uneasy because he had intruded so closely to its nest.

Dr. Newton was familiar with the swamp. He wasn't too worried about alligators. He made plenty of noise as he trudged along. Most gators would avoid contact with a human unless they were cornered. They possessed excellent senses of hearing, smell, and sight, and any he might have encountered would scramble away before he drew too close.

Unless they were very hungry . . .

As he walked, he heard the sound in the trees behind him again. It was closer this time. And then a strange call cut through the darkness . . . not exactly like a gator, but similar. It was the reaction in the swamp to the animal's cry that unnerved him most. Birds that had been nesting screeched in alarm and took to the sky. Off in the distance, he heard alligators calling to their young and the answering squeaks of their babies as they scrambled to find their parents in the darkness. He heard the unmistakable rustle of small animals scurrying away through the underbrush, and other creatures splashing into the water.

And behind him, he heard the same rustling in the treetops again.

Dr. Newton quickened his pace.

And so did whatever was following him.

This part of the swamp was thick with trees, and the ground was soft and marshy, but he ran, grunting and groaning with the effort as he hurtled across the uneven ground. Several times he stumbled, his feet becoming tangled in roots and grasses.

After running for several hundred yards, he stopped to rest and listen. At first he thought he was safe, that whatever was there had abandoned the chase. But the chirping insects and frogs went silent a few moments later as his pursuer caught up. The rustling was back and it was closer this time.

It was right above him.

Dr. Newton sprinted away. He heard something big crashing through the trees behind him. It caught up to him far too quickly. He risked a glance over his shoulder and screamed in alarm.

Flying through the air, its four legs spread wide, the beast glided toward him. Its long neck and large mouth, full of sharp, pointed teeth, made it look somewhat like an alligator . . . but not quite. Dr. Newton saw it silhouetted in the moonlight and let out a bloodcurdling scream.

Having been locked up and drugged for several days, Dr. Newton believed in that moment he was hallucinating. It was the only explanation.

Otherwise, he was about to be eaten by a dragon.

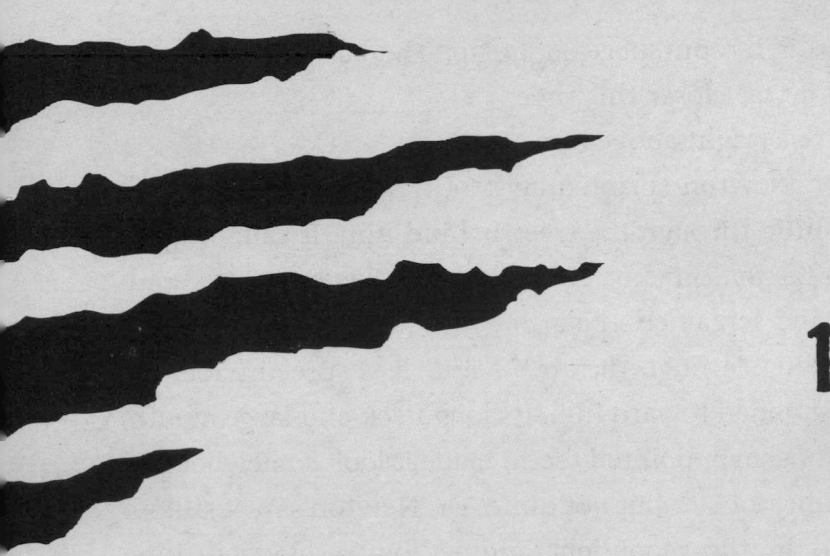

18

EMMET WAS SURPRISED THAT THEY MADE IT OUT OF THE gym, convinced as he was that they were going to die inside it. The only thing preventing him from doing a happy dance was the fact that the hallway was full of Blood Jackets as well. Maybe even more than there were in the gym, if that was possible.

"Where in the world did all of these things come from?" he shouted over the noise of the fire alarm. A Blood Jacket flew at him, landing on his football helmet, and Raeburn deftly flicked it off with her stick.

"Probably nested in the ventilation system," Calvin said matter-of-factly as he swatted another creature that was headed for Riley out of the air.

"Really, Captain Obvious?" Emmet complained. "So, which way do we go?"

Tasker Middle School was designed like a giant letter H. They were in the hall outside the gym. It connected the two large hallways that ran parallel to each other. If they went to their right and then left down the main hallway, they could exit the building and hopefully escape these horrifying creatures.

"This way," Riley said. "There's an emergency door right around the corner."

They followed her lead and went left instead. Emmet was thinking it was smart of her to remember the fire doors. TO BE USED IN THE EVENT OF AN EMERGENCY, the signs said. He was pretty sure this qualified.

They scrambled around the corner and sprinted to the door. The flying death machines followed them, screeching through the air. Calvin charged headlong at the door and grabbed the handle, coming to a crashing, thudding halt.

"Oof!" he said as blundered into it. He pushed the bar again, and nothing happened.

"Somebody sealed it shut," Emmet said, pointing. The handle had been secured with a nylon zip tie.

"Who would do that?" Calvin said.

"It's Dr. Catalyst! He's here!" Emmet shouted.

"You don't know that," Calvin said.

"Yes, I do. My Dr. Catalyst sense is tingling. Who clsc would do this? Come on, we've got to get out of here."

The four of them ran down the hall to the next emergency exit, only to find it was also sealed. Emmet swung his stick at the zip tie in frustration, but it had no effect.

"We need to find something to cut through these. I don't suppose you have a jackknife in your sock?" he asked Calvin.

Calvin shook his head. "You're not allowed to bring knives to school."

"Come on!" Raeburn said. "Let's head to the front door."

They ran back to the center hallway and past the gym doors. Blood Jackets were pouring out of the gym. Emmet couldn't tell if these were new creatures, or if the rest of the crowd had escaped outside and these critters were flying around looking for new victims. It was hard to keep track because they flew extremely fast and there were so many of them looping around one another.

As they reached the other main hallway, they ran to the nearest emergency door. It too was sealed with a zip tie. Someone had deliberately sealed the doors.

"Who would do this?" Riley cried, her voice thick with desperation. The alarm was still blaring.

"Dr. Catalyst!" Emmet insisted. "He's here!"

Calvin and Raeburn began swinging their sticks back and forth while Emmet and Riley tried to find a way to open the door. But without something sharp, it was useless.

"The front door can't be sealed. All of the people at the concert had to get out somehow," Emmet said.

"We can't get out that way," Calvin said. "Look at the doors."

At the front entrance of Tasker Middle School were double doors made with large safety-glass panels on each one. There were tall floor-to-ceiling windows on either side of the doors. Outside, they could see the flashing lights of emergency vehicles, but only barely. The doors were covered with a moving, squirming wall of the hybrid monsters. And more and more of them were flying at the window, trying to escape the confines of the building and the shriek of the alarm.

"Oh. My. God," Riley said.

"We better get out of here before those things notice us!" Raeburn said. She and Calvin were swinging their sticks in a wide arc, trying to keep the nearby creatures at bay. Emmet tried desperately to pry the zip tie loose from the door. He had wedged his stick between it and the door handle, but no matter how hard he pulled, the thick plastic would not give.

"It's no use," he said. "We need to find another way out."

As Emmet tried to work his stick free from the sealed door, a strange feeling came over him. Like he was being watched. And not by the tiny flying death machines. He yanked the stick free and stepped back from the door, looking down the hallway in the opposite direction, toward the rear of the school.

A man was standing there, studying them. He was wearing a black Windbreaker, and though there were plenty of Blood Jackets flying around him, they didn't attack or dive at his head or body. In fact, if anything, they appeared to be ignoring him.

"Look!" Emmet pointed down the hallway, and Riley, Raeburn, and Calvin followed his gaze. The man stared back for just a few seconds, then slipped through the door at the end of the hallway.

"Who was that?" Raeburn asked.

"Dr. Catalyst, I presume," Emmet said. "And I bet he has a way out of here. Come on!"

The four of them sprinted down the hallway in the direction the man had disappeared. They didn't notice that the Blood Jackets that had been covering the windows and doors of the school's front entrance were now alerted to their presence. With a loud shriek, they took to the air and pursued their four victims down the hallway.

19

DR. CATALYST HURRIED THROUGH THE BACK OF THE school. He cursed himself for lingering too long in the hallway. And for forgetting to wear his ski mask, which he now donned. The four kids, ridiculously dressed in football gear, had undoubtedly spotted him. It was a foolish mistake. Once he retrieved the idiot Newton from his futile attempt at escape, he needed to take time and regroup. It would be especially troubling if Calvin had managed to get a good look at him.

There was no time to worry about that now. He had only been visible to them for a few seconds. And he was at the far end of a hallway, with hundreds of Blood Jackets buzzing about. It was unlikely they would be able to identify him.

The end of the hallway held the room that housed the school's electrical systems, heating, and air-conditioning. He stopped at the door. It was a single knob, so there was no way to secure it with one of his zip ties. He looked around for something he might use to jam it but couldn't find anything. If those children were pursuing him, they would be here in a few seconds. He left the door alone.

This area of the building also housed janitorial supplies and various other items needed to operate the school. As he passed the main ventilation duct, Dr. Catalyst could hear the shrieks and the flapping, scratching wings of his creations inside. They must have nested in the cavernous system of air tunnels within the school. Watching them in action had been delightful.

Working his way through the maze of equipment, he reached the door leading to the outside of the school. Carefully, he cracked it open and looked out into the darkness. There was no one around. He slipped outside, and quickly slid a zip tie through the door handle, winding it through a bracket bolted to the doorframe. Let that little snot Emmet Doyle try and get out now.

As he turned from the door he froze, remembering something.

He looked down at the fake FBI Windbreaker he was wearing. The fact that he had made his way into the school for a few seconds and let the kids see him without his face covered did not concern him. Even if Calvin had spotted him, he was far away and they were distracted by the Blood Jackets, and Dr. Catalyst had only been visible for a few seconds.

But he had spoken to the police officer at the front of the school.

If Emmet and Calvin and the others survived, authorities would question them. Undoubtedly they would report spotting someone in the school. Even with a vague description, the police officer might remember that a lone FBI agent claiming to be driving through the area had stopped to offer assistance. The officer was trained to observe, and he had clearly seen Dr. Catalyst's face. Then they could construct a suspect sketch, and an image would be broadcast all over the area, making it more difficult for him to move about and complete his work.

Dr. Catalyst groaned. It was difficult to accept that all of these variables were interfering with his plans. His first Pterogator had been found by one of Dr. Geaux's rangers. Then that cursed Emmet Doyle had shown up, forcing the events that led to the necessity of kidnapping his father. Now he had to deal with that idiot Newton. He almost hoped something in the swamp would eat the buffoon just to shorten his list of chores.

One thing after another had gone wrong. Perhaps

bringing about the type of cataclysmic change he hoped to achieve was too daunting a task for one man.

He closed his eyes and took a deep breath. Ridiculous. He was Dr. Catalyst, brilliant and cunning.

One of the things that had gotten him this far was his photographic memory. It allowed him to remember even the most arcane scientific data. With his talented mind he could recall reams of complex formulas.

It was this very ability that allowed him to remember the name tag on the uniform of the officer he had spoken to earlier. Stukaczowski. The name sounded familiar for some reason, but he couldn't remember why. He would need to be dealt with. And soon. As he thought, Dr. Catalyst worked his damaged arm against his thigh, remembering that moment in the Glades when the Pterogator had turned on him. So much to do. All because of Emmet Doyle.

Just as he was about to slip away into the darkness, he heard frightened screams coming from inside the school, so loud they carried over the sound of the fire alarm. That must be Emmet, Calvin, and their friends, undoubtedly experiencing the singular focus of the Blood Jackets, who would now be driven nearly mad with the need to feed. There was nowhere for the kids to hide.

Dr. Catalyst removed the ski mask and headed for his truck, unable to keep the smile from his face.

20

EMMET AND HIS FRIENDS RAN TOWARD THE DOOR where the mysterious figure had disappeared. The flying monsters were flooding into the hallway. So far, the pads and helmets had managed to keep any of the vicious beasts from getting a serious hold on them. But somehow everyone else had escaped the building. With just the four of them left, the Blood Jackets were refocusing their energies on the only available food source.

Emmet thought the hallway had somehow gotten longer. Why was the end of it so far away now? He realized he was growing tired. Adrenaline and fear would only carry them so far. They must either get out or find somewhere safe to hunker down and wait for a rescue.

"Uh, guys!" Raeburn shouted. "Look behind us."

They slowed and glanced over their shoulders. Emmet immediately wished he hadn't. Hundreds of the Blood Jackets were zooming toward them. They had abandoned their attempt to break through the front door and instead were in full pursuit.

"We're not going to make it," Emmet said. The door to the boiler room was a good thirty yards away, and the creatures were closing fast. This was it. Emmet looked around for anything that might help, or anywhere they could hide. There was nowhere to go. All the classroom doors were locked.

Then his eyes came to rest on the emergency fire equipment. Inside a locked thick glass case was a fire hose. Next to it, also locked behind glass, was a fire extinguisher. As quickly as he could, Emmet swung his hockey stick over his head and brought it down like an axe, smashing the glass covering. He dropped the stick and yanked the extinguisher free from the clips holding it in place. Using it like a battering ram, he smashed through the thicker glass encasing the hose.

"What are you doing?" Calvin asked. He and Riley and Raeburn swung their own hockey sticks back and forth in a mostly futile attempt to keep the flying beasts at bay.

Emmet thrust the fire extinguisher into Calvin's hands. "Here," he said. "Take this and knock the knob off that classroom door. We're going to get inside the room and get out through a window."

Emmet pulled the hose free from its berth in the enclosure. He twisted the valve and heard the hiss of water pressure as the hose immediately filled. He opened the nozzle, spraying water in a wide circle. The Blood Jackets reacted immediately. With shrieks and screeches, they turned and darted away. A few tried to circle back at him, until they encountered the jet of water again and reversed course.

Emmet kept the water moving back and forth like a protective barrier between them and the creatures.

"Hurry up, Calvin!" Emmet shouted. "This isn't going to hold them off forever!"

Calvin swung the fire extinguisher like a club and connected with the doorknob of the closest classroom. It took him several attempts, but the doorknob finally popped free, and the door swung open.

"Come on!" Riley shouted.

The three of them scooted inside the room, and Emmet slowly backed his way toward the door.

"Get ready!" he shouted. "I'm going to drop the hose and jump inside. Get something to hold the door closed."

He backed up closer to the doorway. Water was now covering the floor, and he had to be careful not to slip.

"Ready?" he shouted again.

"Ready!" Raeburn said.

Emmet tossed the hose away and jumped inside the room. He and Riley slammed the door shut and held it closed while Calvin and Raeburn pushed the teacher's desk across the floor and up against the door. A small vertical pane of safety glass was cut into it, and within seconds it was covered with Blood Jackets still trying to get at them.

Emmet looked up at the vent on the wall. So far there was nothing there, but instinct told him it would not be long before they found their way through the vents and into this room. These things were everywhere.

"Let's not wait around!" he shouted.

They crossed the room and cranked open a window. Riley and Raeburn went through first, and Emmet and Calvin followed. Landing on the ground, they tried to stand, but found they couldn't, instead collapsing on the grass in an exhausted heap.

Within seconds police and firefighters surrounded them, lifting them off the ground and carrying them away from the building. Eventually Emmet was loaded onto a stretcher, and he soon saw his dad's face peering down at him.

"Dad! Get Dr. Geaux!" Emmet said.

"It's okay, son. You're okay now," his dad replied.

"No! You don't understand." Emmet sat up on the

gurney and saw Dr. Geaux a few feet away, bent over Calvin.

"Dr. Geaux! It's Dr. Catalyst. We saw him! He might still be in the building. He was headed out the back!"

She stood up and came to his side.

"Who did you see?" she asked.

"A guy in a black Windbreaker and black pants. It had to be him. Those things were swarming all over the place. He must have had some way of keeping them from biting him. Blood Jacket spray or something."

Dr. Geaux pulled a radio from her belt and gave an order for the police to move to the back of the school and to secure all exits from the building.

Emmet lay back down on the gurney. The fire alarm was still blaring in the background. Over it all, he could hear the Blood Jackets shrieking inside the school.

"Dr. Geaux, there's one more thing," Emmet said.

"What is it, Emmet?" she asked.

"I'm quitting Service Club."

21

OVER ONE HUNDRED AND FORTY PEOPLE HAD SUFFERED bites and stings during the Blood Jacket attack on the band concert. More than three dozen people were hospitalized. One was in critical condition after suffering an allergic reaction to the Blood Jackets' venom. He'd been stung over fifty times. Needless to say, the school was closed until the problem with the infestation could be resolved.

"I think I would prefer to be homeschooled now," Emmet said. "Yep. Definitely homeschooled."

He and Calvin, Riley, and Raeburn were at the Florida City Police Department. They'd been treated for bites and scratches, and now all had to join Emmet in getting rabies shots. But in truth, the four of them were relieved. It could have been much worse.

They were gathered in a conference room, seated at a big table. Emmet stood up and walked to the large mirror on the wall. He cupped his eyes and put his face up against it.

"What are you doing?" Riley asked.

"Trying to see through the one-way mirror," Emmet said.

"It's not a one-way mirror," Raeburn said.

"How do you know?"

"Because this isn't an interrogation room," she said.

"And you know that how?" Emmet asked, still trying to see through the mirror.

"I know stuff," Raeburn said.

"They could be watching us, trying to see if we slip up. Don't have our stories straight," Emmet said. He stepped back from the mirror. "You'll never take me alive, coppers!"

Riley and Raeburn laughed and Calvin rolled his eyes. Emmet couldn't help it. He was all nervous and jerky, and felt just like he had the first time he and Calvin encountered the Pterogators in the swamp: like he was going to climb right out of his skin. Ever since he'd arrived in Florida it was one scary critter after another. But being closed up in the school, with no easy way to escape from those things, had really set him off.

The door to the room opened and Dr. Geaux, Emmet's dad, Stuke's father, and a younger woman with a laptop in her arms entered the room.

"Everyone, this is Officer Tracy Mackey," Dr. Geaux said. "She's here from Miami PD and she's going to help us come up with a sketch of the man you saw in the school."

Officer Mackey sat down at the table and opened her laptop. She had shoulder-length curly blond hair and was wearing sharp glasses with black frames. Her smile was friendly and infectious and put them all at ease.

"Okay, Emmet, I understand you were the first one to notice the suspect. What can you tell me about him?" she asked.

"Uh. Not much. I was busy. Being terrified," Emmet said.

Officer Mackey grinned. "I'm sure you were. I can't imagine. But a lot of times, even in tense and scary situations, we see and remember more than we think. Let's start with the simple things first. What was he wearing?"

"He had on a black jacket, like a Windbreaker, and black pants," Emmet said.

"How tall was he?" she asked.

"I don't . . . It was a long way down the hall. Maybe six feet tall," Emmet said.

"And he wore black shoes," Riley chimed in.

"Okay, great! This is all good stuff," said Officer Mackey. "Now, let's think about his face, Emmet. I'm going to ask you to do something very difficult."

Emmet arched an eyebrow.

"Don't worry. I just want you to close your eyes. Can you do that for me?"

"I like to keep them open when I'm not sleeping," Emmet insisted. "Every time I turn around something tries to eat me. It's better if I don't close my eyes."

Officer Mackey laughed, and even Lieutenant Stukaczowski smiled. Ever since his son, Stuke, had been attacked by a Muraecuda, Lieutenant Stukaczowski walked around with a look on his face like he would love to crack apart a bowling ball with his bare hands.

"I understand, but just work with me for a minute," she said. "Close your eyes and don't think about anything but the man at the end of the hallway."

Emmet did as she asked. He closed his eyes, and then opened them again.

"I can't. All I can see are the bats," he said.

"They're not there now." Officer Mackey had a very calming voice. "They've all left the building. It's just you. You hear something, and turn and look, and there's a man. You see his clothing, and now you see his face. What shape is his face? Is it round or narrow?"

"It's narrow," Emmet said.

"Good, now think about the features on the face, his nose and chin. Are they rounded or sharp?"

"Sharp."

"Okay, now his hair. What color is it?"

"It's . . . it's solid black. No. Not solid black. He has gray in it," he said.

"Okay. Can you see his eyes?"

"No. He's too far away. Except . . . wait . . . they're dark colored."

"What about anything else on his face? Did he have a mustache or a scar?"

"No mustache and I don't see a scar."

"Okay. This is good, Emmet. Now, how old would you say he is?"

"Maybe in his fifties. He looks young, but I can tell he isn't. Does that make sense?"

"So he has a young face, not a lot of lines and wrinkles?"

"Yes."

"Now can you — ?"

"The letters," Emmet said.

"What letters, Emmet?"

"On his jacket. When he turned around. They said 'FBI.'"

"Are you sure?"

"Yes. Positive." Emmet opened his eyes. "They were big yellow letters that said 'FBI.'"

"Oh my God," Lieutenant Stukaczowski mumbled. Everyone looked at him.

"What is it, Tom?" Dr. Geaux asked.

"Earlier tonight, I was at the main barricade and a guy approached me. He showed FBI ID and was wearing the jacket. Said he was an agent and was on his way back to Miami when he heard the emergency call on the radio. Wanted to come and lend a hand," he said.

"It was Dr. Catalyst!" Emmet said.

"Let's not jump to any —" Dr. Geaux started to say, but Emmet cut her off.

"It was him! It had to be."

"Why do you think that, son?" his dad asked.

"Because that hallway was swarming with his stupid Blood Jackets. They were everywhere. But they weren't attacking him. I'll bet he has some way of controlling them. Or at least preventing them from biting him. That guy wasn't scared or anxious. He was calm," Emmet said.

"Are you sure?" Dr. Geaux asked.

"Emmet's right," Raeburn said. "Calvin found us the football equipment and even with that, it was all we could do to keep those things from eating us alive. But he didn't even flinch. And somehow he got through the school and sealed up all the doors. How did he manage that in the middle of that swarm?"

The adults in the room considered it, and seemed to arrive at a silent consensus that Emmet was probably right.

"First things first," Officer Mackey said. "Lieutenant Stukaczowski, if you could take a look at my screen and help me fill in the details. You had the best view of the suspect."

Everyone listened raptly as Lieutenant Stukaczowski gave his description of the man. After several minutes, Officer Mackey looked up from her computer and turned it around. The computer software had doctored the image so that it looked almost like a real person.

"What do you think?" Officer Mackey said.

"I don't know," Emmet said. "It sort of looks like the guy, but he was so far away . . . but . . . it's pretty close." Riley and Raeburn nodded in agreement.

"It's enough for us to get it out to the media," said Lieutenant Stukaczowski. "Can you email it to me?"

Officer Mackey nodded and spun the computer around. Her fingers flew over the keys. "I've just uploaded it to all the local and federal law-enforcement databases, as well as all the South Florida media outlets."

Dr. Geaux sent a text on her phone. "I just authorized

an all-points bulletin through the task force. We're going to get everyone out looking."

Emmet felt a giant sense of relief.

"All right," Dr. Geaux said, "let's get you kids home."

They all stood up and filed out of the room. Calvin remained behind, still seated and staring down at the table.

Emmet stopped at the door and looked back at him.

"Calvin? You okay?"

"Yeah."

"Are you coming?"

Calvin stood up and filed past Emmet into the hallway without another word.

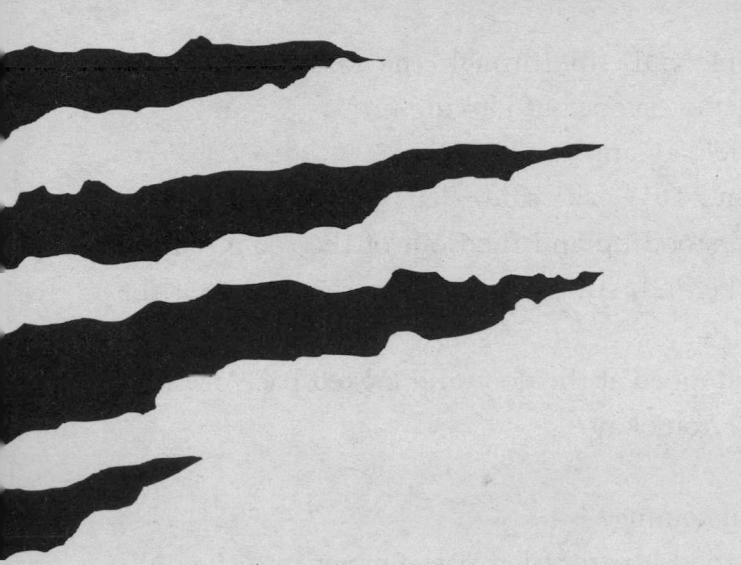

22

HE ALMOST DIED RIGHT THERE.

If he hadn't looked over his shoulder in time to see the Pterogator gliding down on him, it would have been all over but the funeral. Instead, Dr. Newton dived backward into the ground and the creature overshot him. The Pterogator was surprised by the move, thudding onto the grass and rolling with a crash into the underbrush. It gave its loud, roaring cry, and nearby, two nesting cormorants took to the sky in a rush of wings and squawks.

Dr. Newton wasted no time. He took off running in the other direction. The full moon allowed him to see the ground before him. He tried to recall everything he'd learned about the Pterogators. They could glide, and could run on land as fast as alligators. But they were more ferocious. This was not a good situation.

He didn't need to look back to know the beast was coming after him. It was thundering across the ground, crashing through the underbrush and saw grass. Dr. Newton could hear its ragged breathing close behind him. If he could stay ahead of it, run just fast enough that he didn't stumble and fall, it might get tired or find something else to eat.

The Pterogator roared again, and Dr. Newton ran faster. He suddenly emerged from a small shoot of mangrove trees and was happy to find himself on a hard-packed dirt road. Maybe his luck was changing. A road meant civilization of some sort — a house, a ranger station, even a fishing camp. Turning to the southeast, he kept running, staying to the far side of the road, away from the trees. A few yards along and he realized he couldn't hear the Pterogator behind him. It must have given up the chase.

He was wrong.

Ten yards in front of him, the creature burst out of the mangroves and onto the road. Dr. Newton skidded to a halt. The moonlight allowed him to get a good look at the creature. It was terrifying. Its elongated neck was straight up, and it studied him with large, owl-like eyes that shone red.

There was no choice but for him to run in the other

direction. The Pterogator roared again and raced after him. If not for the relatively smooth surface of the road, the beast would have run him down. But his legs were cramping and he was tiring. He needed to get some distance between them. It was run or die.

Just as he was about to break into a sprint, he realized it was quiet behind him. He was about to risk a glance over his shoulder when something heavy crashed into him, knocking him to the ground. Tumbling onto the hard-packed surface of the road, he came to rest on his back. Sharp claws raked over his shoulder and he screamed in agony. He could feel the hot breath of the creature on his face. He looked up to see the Pterogator studying him with its predatory eyes. From this close, the teeth in its mouth looked like hunting knives.

Dr. Newton wiggled and twisted, but the creature outweighed him by several hundred pounds. The beast's clawed forearms were holding his shoulders flat on the ground so that he couldn't breathe. Its claws pierced his flesh again. Dr. Newtown tried to scream, but with no air in his lungs, he found he couldn't even do that.

The Pterogator reared its head back, but before the giant mouth could reach him, Dr. Newton swung his cast-covered arm and connected with the side of the creature's head. The blow startled it. As the most fearsome predator in the swamp, it was probably used to pursuing its food, but once it had the prey in its grasp it would feed without resistance.

Dr. Newton swung again and again. The third time, the plaster cast shattered against the creature's bony head. Momentarily stunned, it rolled to the side, and despite his intense misery, Dr. Newton scrambled to his feet and sprinted down the road. Each step caused searing pain to course through him. Knowing he needed to remain as quiet as possible, he tried everything he could think of to muffle his groans.

But the creature had a sharp sense of smell. It would inhale the odor of blood from his injuries and would not stop pursuing him. Eventually he would drop from blood loss, shock, or exhaustion, and the creature could feed on him at will.

Dr. Newton did not give up. He managed to run a few more minutes with only muffled groans. A quick glance over his shoulder showed nothing. Had he managed to drive it off? Perhaps the blows from his cast had deterred it, and the beast had moved on in search of easier prey.

Dr. Newton's joy was short lived. From the woods to his side, he heard the Pterogator lumbering through the trees. He tried peering through but couldn't get a glimpse of it. In his rapidly weakening state, he couldn't tell if it was running along the ground or flinging itself from tree to tree. Then the Pterogator gave its awful roar, and things went from incredibly bad to monumentally worse.

Ahead of him in the woods, he heard the answering cry of another Pterogator.

Dr. Newton knew from the reports that these hybrid monsters were breeding. It now appeared that the one pursuing him had called to its mate for reinforcements.

Up ahead, the second Pterogator appeared in the road. It was just as ugly and vicious-looking as the other one, which chose that exact moment to emerge from the trees to his rear. They looked at him, their heads darting to and fro, studying him with demonic eyes.

Dr. Newton didn't hesitate. He charged back into the trees. The creatures squawked in surprise and took off after him.

It was difficult to keep track of them over the sound he made crashing through the trees and underbrush. He darted around a cypress and sprinted ahead when one of the Pterogators lunged out of the darkness and snapped at him. It missed, but only barely. If he didn't think of something soon, he was done for. For a moment he considered trying to stay completely still. Predators were attracted by sound, motion, and smell.

Smell.

They could smell him. If he could somehow counter-act their sense of smell, he might have a chance. It was his only hope.

A few yards farther into the woods, a gap opened in the trees. Beneath his feet, the ground grew softer. He sank up to his knees in swampy, muddy water, nearly shouting with joy.

As quickly as he could, he covered his hair, face, and body in a thick coating of mud. He crawled to the edge of the small pit and lay on his back with just his face sticking above the surface. He tried to consciously slow his breathing. Pterogators could hear almost as well as they could see.

The animals called to each other. They were closing in. A few moments later, they glided out of the trees and landed on the ground just yards away. They care-fully sniffed the air, turning in quick circles, their heads leaning one way and then the other as they listened for any sound that might reveal his whereabouts.

One of them put its nose to the ground, as if it were a bloodhound trying to follow his trail. The small marshy bog he lay in was probably fifteen feet across, and the creatures were sniffing the edge of it, understanding the thing they were chasing had been here but now its scent had mysteriously dissipated.

Dr. Newton willed himself to stillness. His shoulders were burning with pain. It felt to him as if someone had poured gasoline on them and lit a match. He closed his eyes, afraid the Pterogators might recognize the two white dots in the mud and launch themselves at him.

All he could do was listen to them grunt and growl as they circled ever closer. One of them huffed and clawed at the muddy bog. Dr. Newton squeezed his eyes shut, preparing for the sharp rake of claws to sever his flesh.

He was unsure how many minutes passed, and whether it was shock or fatigue he couldn't tell, but he suddenly realized that everything was quiet. The insects and frogs nearby began chirping again. Carefully opening one eye, then the other, he looked out to see the Pterogators were gone. Not taking any chances, he didn't move for several more minutes. Then, slowly, and as quietly as possible, he lifted himself to his feet.

The pain and loss of blood made him light-headed, but as he carefully crept through the trees and back to the road, he couldn't help but smile. He had survived a Pterogator attack.

No longer having the strength to run, he plodded along the road. The moon lit his way, riding high in the sky.

Above him in the darkness, several hundred flying shapes crossed through the sky, temporarily blocking the moonlight. Dr. Newton did not look up. He did not see the colony flying along, and did not hear the screeching sound they made when they spotted a lone target stumbling along the road.

They dived toward the ground.

23

AS EMMET LIKED TO POINT OUT, CALVIN WAS QUIET even when he was being chatty. Calvin lay on the bed in his room, staring up at his ceiling in the darkness. Sometimes he wished he were more like Emmet, who was always so certain of his beliefs. And Emmet also took action, even though he pretended to be afraid and incompetent for a laugh. He had gone into the heart of the Everglades after his dad, and he'd rescued Apollo. And on another very important level, he understood what life was like for Calvin. After all, he'd lost his mom.

Calvin's mom tried to get him talking when they returned home from the police station. She had been trying to get him to open up to her ever since he'd come home from the rez in the summer. He loved his mother. She tried so hard, and was smart, and good, and cared about people. And she loved the Everglades almost as much as he did. She didn't know that Calvin knew the park service had offered her promotion after promotion. They had given her the chance to run other parks, or even to move to Washington, D.C. and work there. When he was around the office, he heard other people talking. Calvin was so quiet, he often went unnoticed. But she turned them all down, because she knew Calvin couldn't leave here. It would mean leaving his father behind.

"Are you okay, hon?" she asked, peeking into the door of his bedroom.

"Yeah. I'll be okay. It was pretty hairy though," he admitted.

"I can only imagine. Calvin, I want you to know how proud I am of you. It takes someone very brave to keep a cool head like you do."

He shrugged. Calvin didn't think about things like that. He looked at it more as a case of doing what the situation demanded.

"I guess."

"Listen, son. I know this has been a hard few months and I've been —"

"Mom, really. It's all right. I don't want you worrying about me or Emmet or anything else except finding Dr. Catalyst. I'm fine."

"Do you want to talk about the Green Corn ceremony?"

"Do I . . . uh . . . well. Okay. I was thinking, if it's all right with you, I would ask Uncle Yaha to stand with me. I'd really like it if it could be you, Mom. But the tradition of the tribe . . ."

She tried to keep the disappointment from her face, and failed. Yaha was his grandmother's brother and a tribal elder. A good man, but most of his father's family had been cool to his mother from the beginning of their relationship. It was complicated.

"I think Yaha would be happy to. He's a fine choice." She smiled weakly at him, then closed the door, leaving Calvin alone in his room.

Calvin's grandmother was still alive, but his grandfather had disappeared in the swamp years ago. He'd gone out to hunt and never came back. It happened a lot. The Everglades could be a dangerous place. It had taken his grandfather and his father. His mom told him she always thought the disappearance of Calvin's grandfather was why his father had lived out there. Like he was always looking.

For a kid, losing a parent before it's time is something you never really got over. This summer, while he spent time with his family up at the rez, his father's absence was like an itch he couldn't scratch. Calvin glanced over at the wall, at a photo of him and his dad hanging above his desk. They were with a group of airboat pilots buzzing along out on the River of Grass. Someone had snapped the shot of the two of them, his father at the tiller and Calvin strapped into the passenger seat. His dad had his shoulder-length hair loose, and the wind pulled it behind him like a miniature cape. Calvin still remembered that day. He remembered that exact moment. He didn't think he'd ever been happier.

Emmet popped into his head again. He thought about how much alike and yet how different they were. Calvin admired Emmet and all that he had done. Losing his mom, being jerked all the way from Montana to Florida and plopped down into the middle of all this, he marveled at how well his friend had adapted.

He would never be able to do anything like that. Calvin needed rules. Order. Emmet seemed to thrive in chaos.

And now? Now Calvin didn't know what to do.

Because he'd never told his mom about the photo.

There was a photo in his dad's journal that he'd found in the bottom of the toolbox. His father had tucked it carefully away in the garage. It was a battered old notebook full of his father's observations about the Everglades. There were notes about tides and creeks and compass headings to hidden fishing spots. Jottings about the behavior of birds and animals, and a lifetime of knowledge gained from living out in the River of Grass, the one place Lucas Geaux loved more than any other.

It had drawings and sketches of plants and animals — apparently his father had a talent for art.

And there were some mementoes in the journal as well. A clipping from the tribal newspaper about his grandfather's disappearance, a folded-up copy of his father's high-school diploma, and a photograph.

In the picture, his father was maybe Calvin's age. There was another boy and four men with them, all of them at a camp in the Everglades. Gator skins, freshly caught fish, and even a deer hide stretching on a frame were all laid out in the background. Calvin had studied the photo for many hours. He recognized one of the men as his great-uncle Yaha, but he didn't know the three others, and had never seen any of them on the reservation.

The thing is, he'd never told anyone about the photo. He'd wanted to, but if he did, then he would have to tell someone where he found it. There was no way he could lie. It just wasn't in him. He didn't have Emmet's ability to make up a whopper on the spot.

But the notebook was something between just him and his father. He felt connected to him when he looked through it. And he didn't want anyone to know about it.

At every reservation event, every family gathering he went to, all the picnics and festivals and ceremonies, he had looked for those men. But he never saw them. Not anywhere.

Until tonight.

When Officer Tracy Mackey had finished her Identi-Kit sketch and turned around the computer screen to show them, Calvin recognized him.

He was one of the men in the photo from his father's journal. Calvin had wanted to speak up, he truly did. But he couldn't. If he did, he would have to tell where he'd found the picture. It would mean the only thing of his father's that was truly his, wouldn't be his anymore.

He picked up the photo and looked at it. The man was younger in the picture, obviously, but there was no doubt in Calvin's mind it was the same guy. But who was he? Calvin needed to know.

Quietly, he slipped the snapshot inside his backpack and climbed out his bedroom window. He was going to catch the bus to Everglades National Park HQ, get *THE DRAGONFLY I*, and go find some answers. Calvin left a note on his desk for his mom: "Don't worry. I'm okay. I'll be back." Calvin smiled; if only Emmet were here. He would say, "Dude! That note is so totally you."

The lights were out in the neighboring houses and the street was quiet. When he was certain no one was around, he scurried to the sidewalk and hurried up the street to the intersection and the bus stop.

What he was doing was dangerous. He knew that. But he also understood something no one else did. If he got into trouble — if he didn't make it back — Emmet would find him.

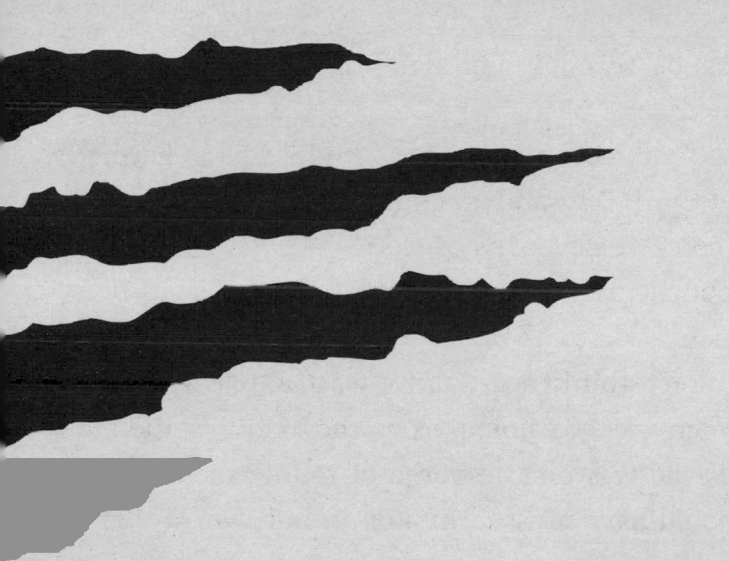

24

"**D**R. GEAUX, HONEST, IF I KNEW WHERE CALVIN WENT, I would tell you. I swear. But I don't."

She had knocked on their door, pounded really, at six o'clock in the A.M., which was seven minutes ago. Emmet was still trying to come fully awake when she'd started interrogating him about Calvin's whereabouts. Thus far, his sleep-addled brain could only determine that his friend was missing, and he'd left a note.

"Was it . . . him?" Emmet asked.

"Him who?" Dr. Geaux asked.

"Do you think Dr. Catalyst . . ." Emmet let the words hang because it was too frightening to even consider.

"No," she said. "Dr. Catalyst didn't kidnap him. He left a note. It's Calvin's handwriting." Dr. Geaux ran nervous hands through her hair and stalked across their living room.

"Rosalita," Emmet's dad said, "I know this is hard. But do you think Dr. Catalyst could have forced him to write the note? To cover his tracks?"

She stopped pacing and let out a big sigh of frustration.

"No! I don't think so. Calvin was acting a little strange when we got home from the police station. Almost like he was on the verge of telling me something. I should have pressed him on it, but I've . . . I'm just so tired."

Dr. Doyle stood and put his arms around her. She slumped against him and tears rolled down her cheeks. Which really scared Emmet. Dr. Geaux was the most fearless woman he'd ever met. She went after Pterogators! If it wasn't Dr. Catalyst, Emmet couldn't imagine why Calvin would do something like this.

"Why would Calvin run off?" Emmet muttered.

"Did you alert the task force?" Dr. Doyle asked.

"Yes," she said. "They're coordinating a search right now. Honestly, Emmet, please don't take offense, but I came straight here. Calvin isn't — he doesn't — he's not as daring as you are and I thought maybe . . ."

"You thought we were off on another one of my hare-brained schemes?" Emmet asked.

Dr. Geaux laughed in spite of herself. "Yes. Forgive me. But yes."

"It's okay, Dr. Geaux. If I were you, I would have suspected the same thing. Did you try tracking his cell phone?"

"First thing I would have done, if it hadn't been sitting on his desk right next to the note," she said. She started pacing again.

Emmet threw himself backward on the couch and looked up at the ceiling. "We need to think like Calvin."

Emmet lay there, the ceiling fan turning slowly. Something had changed. Calvin wouldn't usually do this. Not to his mom. He wouldn't have just taken off without a reason in the middle of a crisis. In Emmet's mind, that meant it was connected to Dr. Catalyst somehow. It was the only thing that made sense.

And what had changed regarding their efforts to capture Dr. Catalyst? The Blood Jackets, but that was nothing new. To Emmet, it felt like Dr. Catalyst was releasing at least one souped-up critter a week. And take last night. While Emmet was busy freaking out in the school, Calvin was his normal, cool-as-the-other-side-of-the-pillow self. Seeing a problem, confronting it, solving it, surviving.

He closed his eyes. In his mind, he went back to the police station. The suspect. In coming up with a sketch, they'd all contributed thoughts and comments: Riley, Raeburn, and Emmet. Not Calvin. But Calvin never said much anyway, so that didn't necessarily point to anything.

Concentrating like Officer Mackey had shown him, he saw Calvin sitting at the conference table, so quiet and still, and remaining there even after everyone else had left the room. The sketch.

"Did you check the *Dragonfly One*?" Emmet asked Dr. Geaux.

"No? Why would he go there?" she asked.

"Can you call? Have someone check? Please?"

Dr. Geaux called a number on her phone and spoke into it. A few minutes later her phone rang.

"Yes," she said. "It's gone?" She stood up. "Patch me through to Manny in Park Ops." She put the phone on speaker, so Emmet and his dad could hear.

"Manny here, Doc. What's up?"

"Manny, did you happen to hear from Calvin this morning? Did he file a float plan with you?"

"No, ma'am. Haven't heard from Little Papi in a while." Emmet remembered Calvin talking to Manny the first time they went out on the airboat. Manny was always cheerful.

"The *Dragonfly One* is gone from the dock; can you pull up the GPS locator?"

"Sure thing, hold on." They could hear the sound of computer keys clicking over the phone. Then again. And again.

"Manny?" Dr. Geaux prodded him.

"I'm checking . . . I . . . Did you say it's gone from the dock?" he asked.

"Yes."

"Well, I'm gonna have to run a system diagnostic because according to the GPS readings it's still right there where it should be," he said. Manny's voice was genuinely puzzled.

"Don't bother with the diagnostic, Manny. I know you keep that system in top-notch condition. I think Calvin removed the GPS unit and set it on one of the other boats."

"What?" Manny asked. "Why would Little Papi do something like that? Did that Catalyst bozo take him? Because if he did, I'll track down that son of a —"

"No. I don't think it was Dr. Catalyst, Manny," Dr. Geaux interrupted. "But can you alert staff at all stations to be on the lookout for him? And get ready to coordinate a grid search; I'm going to be sending out all hands."

"Copy that, Doc. I'm on it." Manny disconnected.

Dr. Geaux looked at Emmet and his dad, and her tears started again.

Emmet almost said something but needed to think more first. The worst thing to do would be sending everyone off on a wild-goose chase. It would take time and it would require him to think like Calvin.

"Calvin," he muttered to himself, "what have you done?"

25

D R. CATALYST KNELT ON THE GROUND, EXAMINING THE remains of a shattered plaster cast. For the first time since he put the idiot Newton in his cell, he felt nervous. How had an imbecile like that managed to escape?

There were signs of a struggle in the nearby grass and bushes. What happened here? Where was his prisoner?

He wasn't worried when he first discovered Newton's escape. The compound where he was holding the teacher was well off the beaten path, a great distance from anything that would offer him either shelter or assistance. Besides, travel on foot through the swamp was full of dangers, not the least of which were his own Pterogators. In fact, it appeared the crafty Dr. Newton may have been too smart for his own good, and perhaps had encountered one of his creations. At the very least, he had met up with a very large predator — an alligator, if not a hybrid.

But while the ground and grasses were crushed and flattened, and the branches on nearby bushes were cracked and broken, and blood was splattered all along the ground, there was no body. Or body parts.

This gnawed at Dr. Catalyst.

Upon first capturing Newton, he had placed a tracking device inside his cast. It was unlikely to be discovered there. And he followed the signal here, to this marshy area near a service road, which was an impressive ten miles from where Newton was kept prisoner. Somehow he managed to make it this far, but the cast was smashed to pieces and he found the tracker buried in the grass.

Dr. Catalyst walked in an ever-widening circle around the spot. His eyes studied the ground, looking for any sign that Dr. Newton might have miraculously gotten up and walked away from this encounter.

A few yards away, he found the traces of someone who'd recently staggered through the undergrowth and followed the trail.

As he walked, he found more blood spattered along the ground. The footprints were erratic, and the person making them had obviously been injured or delirious.

Slowly he developed a new measure of respect for Newton. To have survived for this long was no small feat.

Dr. Catalyst had spent so much time in the swamp that he was completely at home there. Newton was a puffy-haired pseudo-intellectual and should have perished by now. Every minute Dr. Catalyst spent in pursuit of this imbecile kept him from more important work.

Up ahead he came upon a stand of mangrove trees. Dr. Catalyst realized the surrounding swamp had gone quiet and he stopped. The insects and the birds were not just silent, there were none visible. Not anywhere. Strange.

From the trees, he heard a grunting sound.

The branches in the canopy shook.

Dr. Catalyst took a step back, and then several more. The branches rattled again. Then he heard the loud bleat of a Pterogator, confirming his suspicions. Newton *had* encountered one of his creations!

Somehow he'd survived, at least temporarily. But he would undoubtedly be gravely injured. If he was lucky, the idiot would bleed out in the swamp and — presto! — problem solved. But he needed to make sure. He had to find the man or his body.

Or what remained of it.

Slowly and carefully, he backed away from the

Pterogator nest. There was more grunting and shaking from the treetops, but luckily it did not attack. Dr. Catalyst gave the trees a wide berth.

Wanting to be safely away before the animal changed its mind, he finally emerged on the service road. He could see a faint trace of footprints in the hard-packed dirt surface and, every few yards, a small spattering of blood. The morning light was gathering in the east.

He needed to find Dr. Newton soon.

26

EMMET HAD NO IDEA THAT RAEBURN COULD PILOT AN airboat. But as they zipped through the Everglades, he thought, in his inexpert opinion, she was pretty darned good at it. Maybe as good as Calvin.

"If only we had a way to follow him," Emmet said when they'd hatched their plan on the patio at Calvin's house.

"Give me your phone," she said. He handed it over the table with a curious look on his face. Raeburn stood up from the table and stepped into the yard to make a call. She was back in less than a minute.

"We can borrow an airboat from my cousin if we can get to the dock," she said.

"Um. You know how to drive an airboat?" he asked.

"Emmet, dude," she said with a sigh. "I've been *piloting* airboats since I was six."

Emmet thought a moment.

"Okay, we tell Mrs. Clawson we're going to the library . . ." Emmet had to stop a minute to chuckle. Mrs. Clawson was supposed to be watching them as a favor to Dr. Geaux. But she was the worst babysitter ever. "We take the bus to the dock," he said. "Stuke, you're not up to a swamp trip yet. Take my phone and stay at the library. If my dad or Dr. Geaux calls, you answer and tell them I'm in the bathroom or something."

Emmet swallowed hard, just realizing he was making plans for another trip into the Everglades: Land of the Pterogators. This was something he swore he'd never do again. The thought made him sweat a little.

Riley brought supplies in a duffel bag. Bottled water, insect repellent, granola bars, flashlights, and other assorted survival gear.

"How will we avoid the search teams?" Raeburn said.

Emmet held up the portable scanner he'd "borrowed" from the Geaux house.

After Dr. Geaux came to Emmet's house looking for Calvin, she dropped him off at her house so that Mrs. Clawson could keep an eye on him. It was now almost noon and Calvin had been missing since . . . Well, no one knew exactly how long, because he'd snuck out of his house sometime in the middle of the night. Sneaky Calvin. He'd gone rogue.

Emmet asked if it was okay if Riley, Raeburn, and Stuke came over to keep him company. They could at least try to do a group project they were working on for school. It would occupy his mind while Calvin was missing. Dr. Geaux agreed, and they waited until the early afternoon to hatch their plot. By then it was clear Calvin was going to be harder to find than anyone expected.

They gathered on the patio and sat around the table.

"How did you pull this off?" Raeburn asked Emmet. Apollo climbed up in her lap and began a campaign to convince her that he was the cutest dog in the world. It appeared to be working. He lay on his back with paws in the air, enjoying a belly rub.

"Parents never complain when you say you don't want to fall behind on homework. Even though school is closed until they can figure out what to do about the infestation," Emmet said. "And having you guys around *should* keep me from worrying about Calvin."

"You're getting too good at this," Riley said, shaking her head.

Emmet wished they could all be up in the tree house — less chance of Mrs. Clawson overhearing them — but she was in the den with the TV turned up so loud that Emmet doubted she would notice if he decided to jackhammer up the tile in the dining room. Besides, Stuke was still in physical therapy for his leg, and wasn't too confident about climbing yet.

"It required a small amount of deception on my part," Emmet said. "Which I'll admit I feel bad about, but I needed you guys here."

"*Did* he tell you where he was going?" Riley asked, after a pause.

"No," Emmet said. "And we will have a long discussion on that very topic once I get my hands on him."

Raeburn cocked her head, looking at him quizzically.

"What?" Emmet asked.

"You really don't know where he is?" she asked seriously. Emmet didn't like the searching look she was giving him. Leave it to a girl to make you feel like you're under a microscope. He honestly didn't know anything, but she was still making him feel guilty. How did girls do that?

"No, honestly," he said. "This is all Calvin's deal, which is why it's so upsetting. I'm the reckless one. Unless he's being attacked by a horde of Blood Jackets, or about to be eaten by a Muraecuda, he's not exactly . . . The word escapes me," Emmet said.

Stuke looked up from his homework. "Proactive?" He waved to his vocab list. Only Stuke was actually concentrating on schoolwork.

"Exactly. Proactive. And I think it has to be connected to Dr. Catalyst somehow," Emmet said.

"What makes you say that?" Riley asked.

"Process of elimination. Up until now, Calvin has only responded to the situation in front of him. He takes whatever action is required at the time. But after spotting Dr. *Crazylyst* inside the school, he disappears? There has to be a connection," Emmet said.

"And what is it?" Raeburn asked.

Emmet slumped back in his chair. "I don't know. Calvin is so private. He barely talks at all. He's not exactly . . ."

"Effusive?" Stuke said, pointing to the vocab list.

"What does that mean?" Emmet asked.

"Gushing and talkative," Stuke answered proudly.

"That's the opposite of Calvin, all right," Emmet said. "You guys have known him a lot longer than me. Where would he go?"

They grew quiet as they thought, but no one seemed to have an answer.

"Hang on here a minute," Emmet said. "I'll be right back."

Emmet walked into the house, past Mrs. Clawson in the den — who completely ignored him — and down the hall to Calvin's bedroom. He walked in and sat down on the end of the bed, scanning carefully around. Like everything else about Calvin, his personal space was neat and precise. Emmet almost grimaced. It wasn't normal for a twelve-year-old boy to have a room this clean. There should be dirty underwear everywhere and it should smell like moldy sweat socks, like Emmet's room did. It reminded him of Calvin's boat. Everything was sparkling and neatly tucked away.

There was a Florida State Seminoles football poster on the wall. A framed poster on the opposite wall showed the biggest gator Emmet had ever seen, swimming in some canal with a deer in its mouth. A whole deer! It seemed like a very poor choice for a bedroom poster to Emmet.

"That's just wrong," he muttered. "Why constantly remind yourself of something that could eat you and lives right outside your window?"

The desk was empty except for a lamp and Calvin's phone. Dr. Geaux had told him there were no calls or recent text messages in the log. On the wall just above the desk hung a photograph of what must have been his father and Calvin as a young boy. They were in an airboat, zipping along the water in the Everglades. Calvin had a look of pure, unadulterated joy on his face. Looking at the picture made Emmet a little sad. He'd never seen Calvin smile like that.

Emmet lifted the picture off the wall and studied it closely. Calvin was like a smaller version of his dad. He must have been five or six years old when it was taken, and since then his features had changed a little. Emmet thought his friend actually looked more like his mom now. But back then, he had been a miniature Lucas Geaux. But there was something else familiar about the man's face.

Emmet was pretty sure he'd seen it in the hallway of Tasker Middle School the other night.

Older, a little more wrinkled, and the hair was not as long or dark. But it was the same face he'd seen the night they were attacked by the Blood Jackets.

He left the room, hurrying back to the patio. Emmet sat the picture frame down in the middle of the table. Stuke, Riley, and Raeburn all looked at it with interested eyes.

"Does that guy look familiar?" he asked.

Raeburn and Riley both shook their heads.

"No," Riley said.

"Look closer," Emmet prodded.

"What are we looking at?" Riley asked.

"You don't think that's the same guy we saw in the school the other night?" Emmet asked.

"No way," Raeburn said, before Riley could answer. Stuke, of course, had missed the excitement, a point that made Emmet bitter.

"Why 'no way'?" Emmet asked.

"One, that's Calvin's dad, Lucas Geaux," Raeburn said. "He's dead. And two, that's Calvin's dad, Lucas Geaux. There's no way he'd be Dr. Catalyst."

"Why?" Emmet was generally curious.

"You've got to understand something," she said. "When Calvin's dad died, it was kind of a big deal on the rez. Lucas Geaux is *still* a legend in the River of Grass."

"Legend for what?"

Riley and Stuke were sitting in their chairs, watching the conversation between Emmet and Raeburn flow like a tennis match.

"For . . . everything! In the tribe he's — well, let's just say he's revered. He wasn't officially involved in tribal politics as a leader or anything, but he knew more about the Everglades than anyone alive. Probably before or since. He was a guide, a hunter, a fierce protector of tribal lands and rights. He could make an airboat sit up and dance, and he — there's just no way he's Dr. Catalyst. Besides, he died in a crash."

"Dr. Catalyst faked his death in a crash, and he's alive," Emmet said. "And Dr. Geaux told me Lucas's body was never found."

"I know, but it's not him," Raeburn said. "Trust me. Somebody dies in an accident out in the Glades — they don't find the bodies. The gators, every critter with teeth finishes 'em off if they don't sink into the swamp.

Besides the guy we saw was older than Calvin's dad would be. On top of that, he would never leave his family. He died, Emmet. You need to look elsewhere."

"You said he could 'make an airboat sit up and dance.' Well, Dr. Catalyst used an airboat to fake his death, too! You don't find that a little convenient?"

"It's a coincidence. Do you know how many airboats crash in the Glades every year? How many fatalities? They don't publicize it, because it hurts tourism, but there are a lot of accidents. Besides, Lucas Geaux would never leave his family willingly."

"Why?"

"It's just not done. In the Seminole culture, family is the center of everything."

"Dr. Geaux also told me that him marrying outside the tribe was not well received by his family," Emmet said.

"I don't know about that. I just know people still talk about him, and he loved the Everglades, and —"

"Exactly," Emmet interrupted. "That makes him the perfect Dr. Catalyst."

"Except you're forgetting something," Raeburn said.

"What?"

"Think." She smiled at him, but Emmet was stumped. Riley picked up the picture and studied it for a moment.

"I think Raeburn is right," she said. "The guy in the hallway looked older to me. The math doesn't work.

This guy is in his early thirties. If Calvin was five or six when this was taken, his dad would be like forty now. The guy we saw was in his fifties, at least. Maybe older."

Emmet slumped back in the chair and looked at Raeburn.

"And if Calvin's dad is still alive," he said, "he probably doesn't have the scientific knowledge to create hybrid species."

Raeburn smiled and nodded.

"I still think there's a connection somehow," Emmet said. "Calvin went to find it."

"So let's go find him," Raeburn said.

And that's how they came to be rushing through the swamp looking for Calvin, with only a couple of hours before they had to get back. Stuke waited dutifully at the library with Emmet's cell phone. Emmet had taken Calvin's off the desk. Raeburn knew Lucas Geaux's old camp was up in the Shark River Slough, near the mouth of the Broad River, and that's where they headed. It wasn't being searched yet, and was as good a place as any to start looking.

Everything was going fine until the boat broke down.

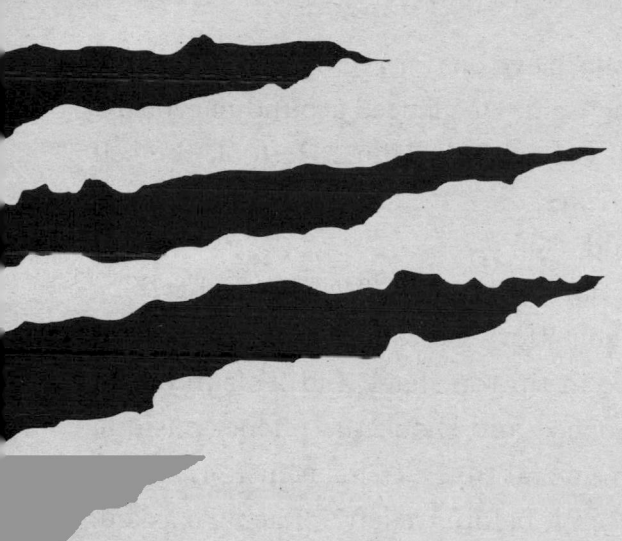

27

"**U**M, RAEBURN, WHY IS THE BOAT NOT WORKING?" Emmet asked. The engine had just gone dead with a series of hacks and sputters. They were now floating slowly across the water's surface.

"I don't know, Emmet," she said.

"Can you fix it?" Riley asked.

"I don't know, Emmet," Raeburn repeated. She opened the engine cover and peered inside.

"Where are we?" Emmet asked.

"The Everglades," Raeburn said absentmindedly as she peered into the compartment.

"Is that supposed to be funny?" Emmet snarked.

"Not particularly. One thing at a time," she said.

"Riley, keep a sharp eye out for Pterogators and those bat things," Emmet said. He glanced around nervously. "I'm going to kill Calvin. Kill. Him." He took the cell phone from his pocket.

"Oh, no," he said.

"Don't say 'oh, no,'" Riley said. "'Oh, no' what?"

"The phone. The battery is dead. Calvin isn't around to keep his phone in tip-top shape and it's run out of juice." Emmet groaned and shook the phone, pushing the power button several times. "This is just great."

"You didn't check it before we left?" Raeburn asked. She removed a long piece of tubing from the engine and examined it in the light.

"Why would I check? It's Calvin's phone. It's always fully charged," he said.

"That's true. Calvin is very good about maintaining anything mechanical," Raeburn said. She blew through the small rubber hose, watching in disgust as a big glop of sludge and dirt emerged from the other end. "Unlike my cousin, apparently."

"So what's wrong?" Emmet asked hopefully.

"Clogged fuel filter is my guess. I'll have to see if I can get it free and clean it so it will run long enough to get us back," she said.

A bull gator bleated from somewhere in the nearby saw grass, and Emmet nearly jumped out of his skin.

"Relax," Raeburn said. "It's not a Pterogator. Just a normal one."

Riley and Emmet had no choice but to sit and watch as Raeburn tried fixing the engine. She was diligent in her work, mumbling to herself as she toiled for a few minutes, then tried starting the boat. It didn't work. The motor would not turn over. She stuck her head down in the engine compartment again.

"I think I've got it," Raeburn said.

Emmet realized he was really sweating. Not just because of the heat and humidity, but because he didn't like being out here. He was working on some choice takedowns for Calvin when they found him.

"You can get the boat moving?" Riley asked excitedly.

Raeburn opened a panel along the side of the boat's deck. She removed two plastic paddles. "Yep," she said, holding them out to Riley and Emmet.

"What?! You can't be serious," Emmet said.

"I'm completely serious," Raeburn said. "We paddle back to the mouth of Broad River and float downstream, then hopefully we can pick up a tow from someone."

"Hopefully?" Emmet said.

"We don't really have much choice," Raeburn countered.

"I guess not," Emmet said. "But why aren't you paddling?"

"Do you know how to steer an airboat?" Raeburn asked.

"No," Emmet groused. He took the paddle, and he and Riley knelt on opposite sides of the deck, near the bow. They dipped their paddles in the water, and after a difficult heave, the boat moved slowly forward.

"This is going to take forever," Emmet said. "And we're not any closer to finding Calvin."

"We're not likely to find him with a broken-down airboat," Raeburn said.

Emmet put his back into paddling. They worked hard for about a half hour, until he and Riley needed a rest. When Emmet looked up, he saw the sun was moving lower in the sky, now just above the treetops to the west. This made him a little nervous. Actually, it made him completely frantic. But he tried not to show it.

"How much farther until we hit the river?" he asked Raeburn.

"Probably another quarter mile," she answered.

"It's getting dark," Emmet said.

"Then you should paddle faster, and talk less," Riley groused.

"I don't like the dark. At least not in Florida," Emmet said. As if to remind him why, they heard the bleating of another bull alligator from somewhere nearby. Emmet dug his paddle into the water and pulled like his life depended on it. He tried hard not to think about his life depending on it.

Finally, they reached the river and, with some tricky maneuvering, were able to turn themselves south, back toward civilization. But they weren't safe yet. Emmet and Riley paddled as Raeburn steered, and the current carried them a bit faster.

But not fast enough.

The sun continued sinking behind the trees, and the sky darkened. None of them said it, but they were all thinking the same thing. Nightfall meant Blood Jackets.

Emmet felt foolish. All he'd wanted to do was help Calvin. Now they were going to be trapped in the swamp like sitting ducks. It was his fault.

They each looked up as the noise of hundreds of leathery wings rushing into the night sky reached their ears. And then came the same high-pitched screeches they'd heard in the school.

The Blood Jackets were coming.

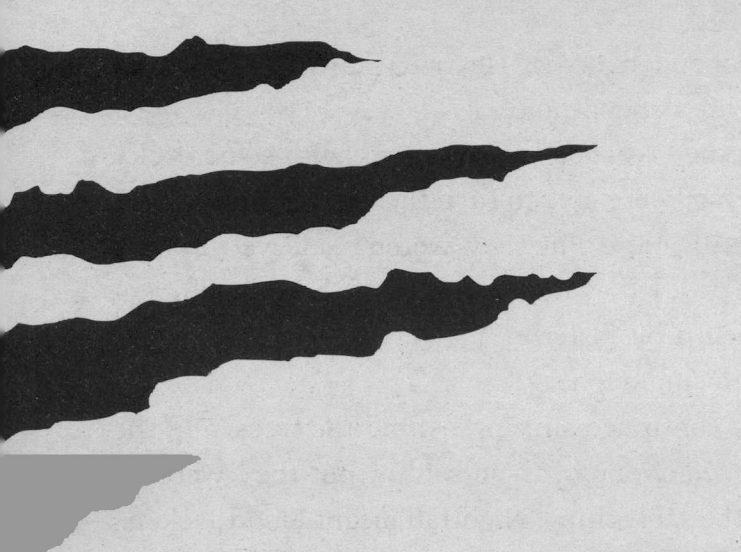

28

A GRAY PICKUP SKIDDED TO A STOP ON THE GRAVEL DRIVE in front of a deserted hotel. Dr. Catalyst hopped out of the cab and hurried inside. Once there, he gathered his equipment and gear and loaded it up. The trip to the swamp was a disaster. Try as he might, he was unable to find that fool Newton anywhere.

It had been relatively easy to follow the trail Newton left on the road. At some point during his escape, the man appeared to have been running, for his footprints were very far apart. At some point his tracks had become scattered all over the surface of the road and then disappeared back into the swamp. Dr. Catalyst had lost the trail in the marshy bogs that lined the service road.

He took a deep breath, trying to calm his nerves. Even if Newton had somehow miraculously survived, it was unlikely he would remember anything incriminating. And this particular base was unknown to anyone. Truthfully, he couldn't bring himself to believe the man was alive. There were just too many dangers in the Everglades. It was hard to imagine a dolt like Newton could survive.

Still, it was vital he remain free, in order to continue his work saving the Everglades. So far he had avoided capture by taking no chances. With Newton at large, he would need to go to ground again, and there were plenty of places for him to hide. He could afford to wait until Newton surfaced, or it was confirmed he'd perished. If he was still alive, he could be dealt with then.

His equipment and supplies were what was important now. He never traveled with many personal effects — a few changes of clothes in a small duffel bag and some toiletries were all he carried with him. It allowed for escape at a moment's notice.

After he loaded everything into the truck, he returned to carefully check that he'd left nothing behind. Everything was accounted for.

Once back on the road, Dr. Catalyst tuned the radio to check the local all-news station. The newscaster was already midway through a report about a search now taking place in the Everglades. Dr. Catalyst nearly drove his truck off the road. Were they out there looking for Dr. Newton? How could this be? Who could have possibly determined that was where he had taken his captive?

He turned up the volume and listened carefully. He almost wrecked again when the announcer said that Dr. Geaux's twelve-year-old son, Calvin, was believed to be missing in the Everglades.

Calvin was missing!

Dr. Catalyst turned off the road into the parking lot of a vacant gas station. He waited for the traffic to clear and then zoomed out onto the highway, speeding as fast as he could toward the Everglades.

29

Emmet was momentarily frozen as he watched the horde of Blood Jackets flood the night sky. There must have been a nest nearby. They soared into the darkness a fair distance away, but their cries echoed through the air. The creatures circled above their nest, as if the sky was filling with the entire colony. They dipped and darted, swirling through the air as they took off in search of prey.

It did not take them long to discover three humans on a broken-down airboat.

"Paddle! We've got to move!" Emmet said. Over and over he pushed the plastic oar through the water, grunting with the effort.

"There's nowhere to go, Emmet!" Raeburn said.

"There has to be somewhere! Can we crawl in the engine compartment?"

"It's too small!" Raeburn shouted.

The creatures were coming closer.

"We can go into the water!" Riley shouted as she paddled.

"No way! There's Pte — No way."

"We can't outrun them!" Raeburn said.

Emmet glanced in every direction, hoping against hope that a secure, impregnable Blood Jacket–proof shelter would suddenly appear in the middle of the swamp. Or a phone booth. Even a cardboard box. Then he saw their only chance.

"Raeburn! Over there! Those mangrove trees! Hurry!" Emmet said.

They paddled frantically as Raeburn maneuvered the tiller. The trees rose up out of the water like giant dandelions. Their roots, bent and gnarly, wormed their way into the water like the fingers on a witch's hand. Emmet peered over his shoulder and could see the cloud of flying creatures in hot pursuit.

"Faster!" Emmet shouted.

They crossed the last few feet to the trees, and the airboat bumped gently against the mass of tangled, twisted branches.

"We've got to climb inside the roots!" Emmet said, leaping out of the boat and scrambling toward the clump of trees. A few Blood Jackets were swarming around now. The main body of the colony was almost upon them. Swinging his paddle, he connected with a few of them, knocking them into the water.

"Hurry!" he said.

Riley and Raeburn wasted no time jumping out of the boat and wiggling their way into the mass of roots, groaning with the effort. Emmet followed after them. They burrowed into the roots as far as the space would permit them. It had been a moment of desperation, but Emmet was relieved to find that the twisted roots provided at least some protection from the Blood Jackets.

He held on to his oar, using it to poke away the more determined bloodsuckers — those whose hunger drove them mad enough to reach the three of them.

"How long do we have to stay here?" Riley asked.

"I don't know," Emmet said. "Hopefully they'll take off soon to hunt for something easier to catch." He wielded the oar like a spear, working into the spaces between the roots and shoving the creatures away.

The colony covered the trees and their roots, trying every way they could to breach the wooden cage that held a ready meal. One of them stung Raeburn on the hand before she batted it away.

"Ow!" she cried.

It came at her again and Emmet jabbed it away with the oar. More and more Blood Jackets piled onto and around the trees. Before long, the three friends couldn't see anything but flying fangs trying to get at them. The noise of their screeching and flapping was deafening.

Then, without warning, the colony flew away all at once.

The bats were there and then they were gone, rising into the darkening sky as one. The three of them watched, staring in openmouthed wonder as the creatures disappeared, their cries fading into the night.

"I wonder what made them leave," Raeburn said.

A noise issued from out of the water. It was one Emmet had heard before, a few times in person, and many in his nightmares. It focused their attention on the shore, a few short yards away from the trees. There was just enough light remaining to see the outlines of two elongated reptilian heads rising from the surface of the water. Two pairs of reddish eyes, glowing with menace, stared directly at them.

"Pterogators . . ." Emmet choked.

30

THE PTEROGATORS ROARED AT THE SAME TIME, trumpeting loudly into the night. Their heads snapped back and their large red eyes locked on to the mangrove trees. As they swam forward, their heads darted beneath the surface, lost from view.

"Oh no, oh no, oh no," Riley said.

"Where did they go?" Raeburn asked.

"Probably went in the oppo — Gahhh!" Emmet shouted as the two Pterogator heads popped up out of the water directly in front of them. "Here! They came right here!" Emmet shrieked.

Both of the creatures left the water, pulling themselves onto the mass of roots. One tried reaching through the twisted tangles with a forearm, and Emmet jabbed it away with the oar.

"Get out of here!" he shouted.

The Pterogator drew back, roaring again, confused by Emmet's action. The three of them screamed then, as its open jaw snapped forward, biting off several chunks of the mangrove roots. The teeth and jaws of the creature were only inches away. The Pterogator backed up and lunged forward again, jaws snapping. Emmet shouted and jammed the oar forcefully into the Pterogator's mouth. The beast crunched down, snapping off a big chunk of the oar, and shook its head from side to side.

"I hope you choke on it!" Emmet screamed.

He looked at the remaining stub of oar in his hand.

"Probably shouldn't have done that," he said.

"We need to get out of here," Raeburn said.

"Are you crazy?" Emmet said.

"What do we do? Wait until it chomps its way in here?" Raeburn answered back.

Emmet was about to speak when the Pterogators roared again and stood up on their rear legs, their jaws snapping. At first, Emmet couldn't understand what was happening, but then he heard the chittering noises and flapping wings of the Blood Jackets.

They were attacking the Pterogators.

Wave after wave of Blood Jackets swarmed over and around the two lizards. With mighty roars, the reptilian hybrids snapped their jaws, catching the small flying beasts in their teeth. Their skin was too thick for the Blood Jackets to pierce or sting, but the smaller creatures would not relent so easily.

"What are we going to do?" Riley shouted.

"What can we do?" Emmet said. "I just hope they tire each other out."

The Blood Jackets shrieked and the Pterogators bellowed, and for a moment Emmet felt like he was watching some kind of horror movie. But it was no movie. It was real.

All they had to defend themselves was Riley's oar. Even the airboat had been dislodged from the shore and had floated off.

It was almost too dark to see, but Emmet sensed Raeburn moving.

"Come on," she said.

"What? 'Come on' where?" Emmet asked.

"We need to work our way to the other side of this copse of trees while they have each other occupied," she said.

The trees made a small clump in the water that was maybe fifty or sixty feet in diameter. She wiggled her way through and around the roots, until she emerged from the tangled mass at the side farthest from the fighting monsters.

"Raeburn, that's crazy, you're — Look out!" Emmet shouted.

A group of the Blood Jackets had sensed her presence, no doubt reading the heat from her body. As they swarmed around her, Raeburn jumped from the trees into the waist-high water and went under. The hybrids squealed and fluttered over the spot where she disappeared, but quickly flew away to rejoin the attack on the Pterogators.

Raeburn's head popped up out of the water.

"Come on!" she said. "We can get to the boat this way!"

Over the growls of the fighting animals, Emmet heard a new sound, something like a motor. No. It was exactly like a motor. All of a sudden, an airboat pulled into view and a spotlight shined over the water where Raeburn stood. The Blood Jackets attacked the light.

Someone stood at the tiller in a black coverall, wearing a helmet.

"Get on! Hurry!" said a muffled voice.

There was no other option. If they stayed, they would perish.

Raeburn had already scrambled aboard. Riley and Emmet maneuvered their way out of the twisted roots to the far side of the trees. They splashed through the water and swung their hands wildly around, keeping the flying hybrids from reaching them. The Pterogators were still occupied by their own attackers.

Splashing through the water, Emmet and Riley reached the side of the boat and scrambled over, sprawling on the deck.

The pilot opened the throttle and the boat practically leapt in the water. The moon was coming up and lighted their way as they zipped across the swamp. At their speed, they easily outpaced the Blood Jackets, who gave up the chase.

Emmet managed to gather himself and helped Riley to her feet. After they had outrun the horde, the boat slowed and the engine quieted to an idle.

It occurred to Emmet that they had jumped onto a strange airboat in the middle of the Everglades. For all he knew, it could be Dr. Catalyst standing at the tiller. But he didn't think so.

"I'm glad I found you," the pilot said. He removed the helmet. It was Calvin.

"Oh, hey, Calvin," Emmet said, nonchalantly wiping a glob of swamp gunk from his face. "We were just looking for you."

Calvin nodded. "I have something to tell you," he answered.

"I hope it's 'Sorry I abandoned you guys and disappeared into the swamp'?"

"Better get everyone buckled in first," Calvin said.

Riley and Raeburn took the seats and buckled in. Emmet stood next to Calvin's pilot chair and held on to the metal frame.

"So, what is it?" Emmet said.

"I know who Dr. Catalyst is," Calvin whispered to Emmet.

Emmet's eyes went wide, but before anyone could ask another question, Calvin opened the throttle and *THE DRAGONFLY I* leapt across the water.

Headed for home.

FROM DR. CATALYST'S FILES
"Blood Jacket"

Unquenchable hunger for blood

Piercing stinger

Six spindly legs

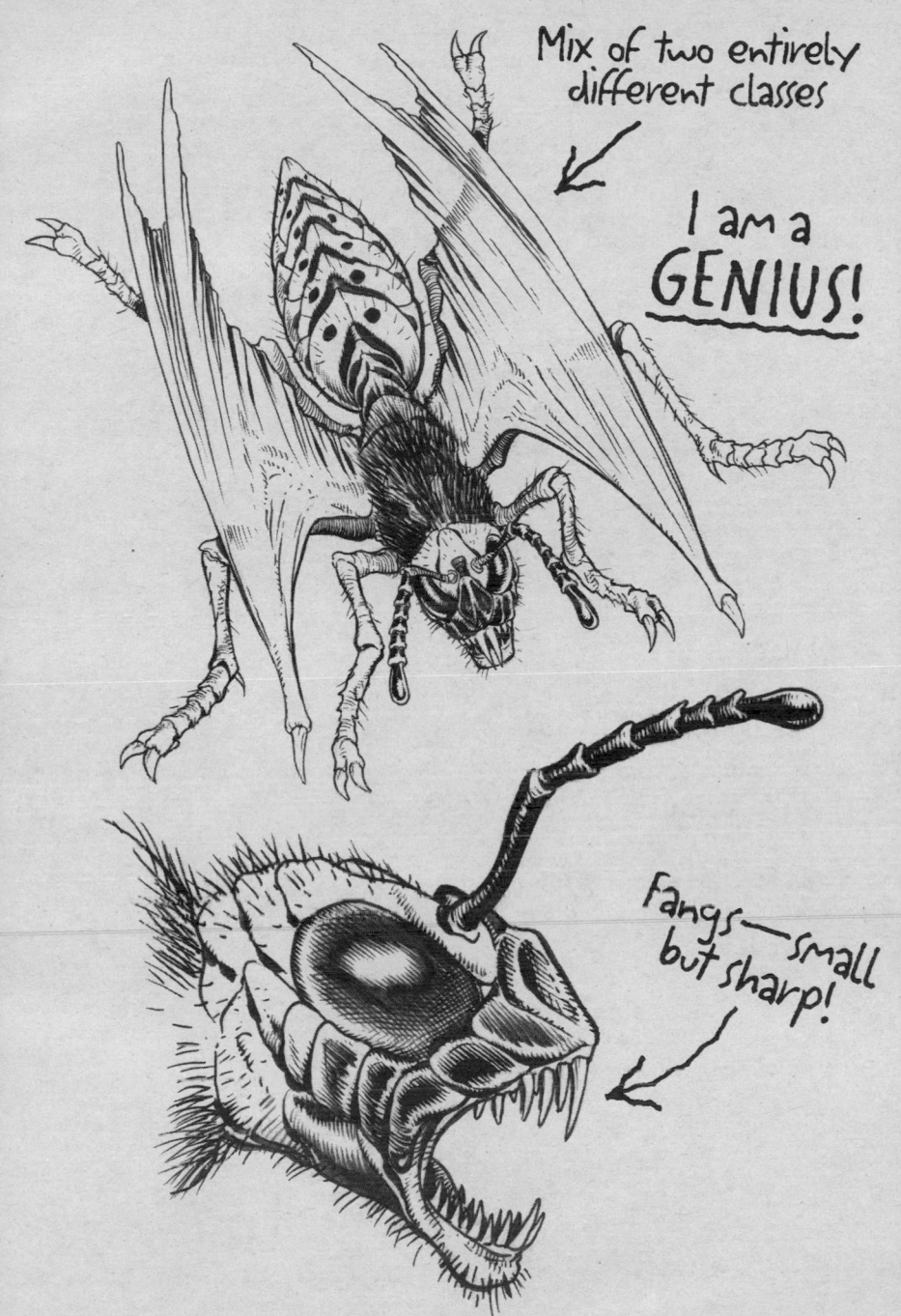

A sneak peek of the next
K|LLER SPEC|ES

ultimate attack

IT WAS STILL SO HARD FOR HIM TO ACCEPT.

Up until this moment, almost everything had gone wrong. Unexpected forces were aligned against him. Variables not considered in his equations and simulations somehow appeared with regularity. There was no doubt about it: Dr. Catalyst's plan to restore the Florida ecosystem was coming apart at the seams.

Everything that could go wrong did. One by one, his Pterogators were being gathered up in the Everglades. While their introduction dramatically reduced the snake population, they had not eradicated the pythons and boa constrictors as he had hoped. His Muraecudas put a severe dent in the number of lionfish on the coastal reefs. But apparently they'd migrated to other waters, or had perhaps fallen victim to sharks or bigger predators. None had been sighted in weeks, and the lionfish were returning.

And the media was reporting that his Blood Jackets, which he considered his crowning achievement, were dying off. Scores of them had been found dead all over Florida City and the surrounding countryside. He hadn't even been able to recover the body of the inept Dr. Newton from the swamp. Surely the man was dead, but it was a loose end, and Dr. Catalyst did not like loose ends.

It felt as if he were teetering on the brink of total failure. Early on in his campaign, he had issued a manifesto. Sent to hundreds of media outlets and posted online, it called for like-minded individuals to join his efforts. It was his hope to start a movement, to rally others to his side. It had utterly failed. No one had offered to join him. A few fringe environmental groups had "endorsed" his efforts, but Dr. Catalyst had envisioned throngs of people — hundreds, if not thousands — flocking to his cause. They never materialized. The media called him a crackpot and a danger to society. How preposterous.

He was a visionary.

Still, despite his genius, his efforts had not had the desired effects. And there was one reason. In his mind, his creatures would be healing the fragile Florida ecosystem right now if not for the harassment and interference of a particular individual.

Emmet Doyle.

When the Doyle brat showed up — that was when his plans had gone awry. Someone not even old enough to shave was dashing his hopes and dreams for a naturally restored Florida Everglades. Interfering. Agitating. Forcing him to divert his precious time and resources from his mission. And now he was left with no other choice but to remove this obstacle. No matter the cost.

Prior to releasing his creatures, Dr. Catalyst had purchased over two-dozen vehicles. It had been comically simple for someone of his brilliance to hack into the Florida Department of Motor Vehicles registration database and create false registrations and titles of ownership for each vehicle.

One of them, a dark brown panel van was parked at the curb a few hundred yards down the street from the Doyle home. The windows on the rear door were tinted, allowing no one to see inside. A few ventilation slots were cut into the vehicle to allow air to circulate. The name of a famous national delivery service company had been painted on the side. The van's license plate and registration would easily pass muster if he were to meet a police officer. Provided they did not ask him to open the rear doors. No one must view his cargo.

That would be a problem.

As if to illustrate his point, the van jerked on its suspension and a strange, growling, laughing roar came from the van's cargo bay. His newest creation was keen to steal into the night. A low growl sounded through the rear wall of the van, and the vehicle bounced again as the creature threw itself against its cage. It was eager to be set free. To hunt.

But patience was required.

At his campaign's start, Dr. Catalyst had placed video and audio recording devices at National Park Service headquarters. It allowed him to keep tabs on the comings and goings of Dr. Geaux and Dr. Doyle, and on their efforts to thwart him. Somehow they had discovered he was monitoring them and staged a futile attempt to capture him by feeding him false information. He had easily seen through their feeble deception. However, they had removed his surveillance equipment. Now he no longer had inside information on the movements of his enemies.

Dr. Catalyst paused mid-thought. He could hear muffled growls and groans from the animal in back. The van shook again as the creature launched itself repeatedly at the side of its cage. He had not fed it yet today, deciding that hunger would hone its hunting instincts.

Finally the animal quieted. Dr. Catalyst resumed watching the street.

The loss of his equipment forced him to resort to actual physical observation. He couldn't trust replacing the bugs at the park offices or on Doyle's and Geaux's vehicles. They were now regularly checked for listening devices. So he did it the old-fashioned way. Trailing them around town. Spying on them whenever he could do so unobserved, until he had enough data on their routine behavior for his next grand demonstration.

It took precious time away from his work, but eliminating Emmet Doyle would also remove Dr. Doyle and Dr. Geaux from the equation. Then his mission could continue.

His fleet of vehicles had come in handy as he followed Emmet and his father at various times during the day and night. Tonight was Thursday. On Thursdays Emmet and his father joined Dr. Geaux and Calvin at Pompano's Pizzeria and did not return until after 9 P.M.

Dr. Catalyst looked at his watch: 9:10 P.M. They would be arriving any moment. As if on cue, he saw their pickup truck in his driver's side mirror, turning onto the street. He leaned down in the seat as it passed by, making sure they didn't spot him. A lone man sitting in a van at night might be remembered. An empty vehicle would draw little attention. The truck passed by and continued down the street until it turned into their driveway. He sat up, watching as Emmet and his dad exited the pickup and entered their home.

On the seat next to him sat a pistol filled with an extremely powerful tranquilizer dart. In the unlikely event that the creature in back decided to turn on him, he would need it. Next to it was a cattle prod. Dr. Catalyst was not cruel to animals, nor was he particularly worried it might attack him. It had been engineered and trained to seek out only one prey.

Still, Dr. Catalyst muttered his mantra.

"No chances."

Scanning the street, he confirmed that no one was around. He grabbed the tranquilizer gun and cattle prod, then opened the door. Quietly, he stole toward the rear of the van. Dr. Catalyst holstered the pistol and put his free hand on the door handle. Flicking the switch on the cattle prod, he heard a whirring hum as the device charged.

Dr. Catalyst took a deep breath. Once the rear door was opened, a system of cables and pulleys attached to the cage gate would raise it and his creature would bound from the van.

And it would hunt.

It growled again, and the van shook once more. It was almost as if the creature could sense that it was about to be set free. And it was impatient. Dr. Catalyst pushed a button on a small device attached to his wristband. It sent a signal to a collar the creature wore, delivering a mild electric shock to the beast. From within the bowels of the van, Dr. Catalyst heard a cackling laugh from the animal. The "laughing" sound signified submission to a superior.

What waited inside the pen was his latest hybrid. A singular creation. It was not made to counter an invasive species. It was not born in his lab to prevent the destruction of the Everglades. This beast had one purpose and one purpose only.

To find, follow, and kill Emmet Doyle.

Dr. Catalyst opened the door and heard the squeak of cables and pulleys raising the gate to the metal cage. He stepped behind the van door, peeking around to view the magnificent animal emerge from the dark interior. It strode to the edge of the cargo bay and stood in the open rear doorway. It sniffed the night air, then raised its head and howled its odd and terrifying cry. It was half the laugh of a hyena, and the other half the growl of the Florida panther.

It was a terrifying monster. It had the long tail and strong, thickly muscled rear legs of the panther. The front legs, spotted coloring, and head were all hyena.

Except for the jaws.

The jaws and fangs were a wicked combination of each species. Two rows of razor-sharp teeth emerged from its mouth. It looked as if hunting knives were somehow growing from each jaw.

For a moment, Dr. Catalyst worried the creature

would not leave. It sat on the edge of the van, surveying the night. Ever since his Pterogators were first released, Emmet Doyle had interfered at every turn. After Emmet rescued his father in the swamp, Dr. Catalyst began to prepare for this eventuality. As he nursed his wounds and cursed his fate, he had understood the boy and his father would continue to be a problem. And they had thwarted him at every turn. The only solution to the obstacle was to eliminate it. So he created what now stood there, still and silent. He savored the moment.

Each stage of his experiments produced vast improvements in his gene splicing, recombinant DNA, and accelerated growth methods. Until the Blood Jackets, which appeared to be dying out. He suspected the cause was that the species were too divergent.

But hyenas were a close relative of the feline family — although they resembled dogs, and most people assumed they were canines. Dr. Catalyst was sure this combination of species would be his greatest achievement yet. It had to be. There was too much at stake. Once he had created a predator that could identify, stalk, and eliminate a single target, there would be no limits on the environmental damage he could reverse. With this technique perfected, he could generate an entire species that would cull other invasive species all over the world. Just as the animal in the cargo bay of the van would eliminate Emmet Doyle.

The genes of the panther would create a stalking predator that would fixate on its prey. The hyena genes forged a relentless and fearless hunter. Hyenas excelled at hunting, despite their reputation as scavengers. And they were ferocious in their own right, often driving off much bigger leopards and lionesses from their kills. The look of the animal alone would send terror coursing through Emmet Doyle. Dr. Catalyst's face twisted into a snarl. How he wished he could be there the first time the obnoxious little brat encountered the animal. To see the fear and terror in his eyes would be such a thrill. Instead, he would have to settle for letting this surrogate enjoy the final victory.

The great beast sniffed the air again and Dr. Catalyst pushed the button on the cattle prod, hearing a crackle of electricity as it discharged. He hoped it would not require any convincing to leave. But he would be ready if it did.

But he needn't have worried. Using its powerful hind legs, it leapt from the van and landed deftly on the blacktop. Without looking back, it trotted away. For a brief moment Dr. Catalyst wondered if he would ever see it again. There was a tracking device inserted in the skin beneath its neck, but who knew how long the power would last?

The creature stopped in the middle of the street and inhaled the night air. It paused, shaking its head back and forth, as if trying to focus. Then it caught the scent it desired and loped away into the darkness.

Heading directly for the Doyle home.